I0670435

This Person Is Not

That Person

This Person Is Not
That Person

Who are we when we are with someone else?

Stories

Susan McCreery

PUNCHER & WATTMANN

© Susan McCreery 2019

This book is copyright. Apart from any fair dealing for the purposes of study and research, criticism or as otherwise permitted under the Copyright Act, no part may be reproduced by any process without written permission. Inquiries should be made to the publisher.

First published in 2019
Published by Puncher and Wattmann
PO Box 279
Waratah NSW 2298
http://www.puncherandwattmann.com
puncherandwattmann@bigpond.com

ISBN 978-1-925780-44-4

NATIONAL
LIBRARY
OF AUSTRALIA

A catalogue record for this book is available from the National Library of Australia

Cover images by Alec Hamilton
Typeset and cover design by Jessica Lewis
Printed by Lightning Source

Contents

Previously published

(in earlier versions)

'Eight Seconds' *Writing to the Edge* (Spineless Wonders, 2014)

'The Uninvited' *Lost Boy and Other Stories* (Margaret River Press, 2015)

'Companion Planting' *Island* #116, 2009 (under the title 'Kindness')

'Angie's Sparkle' *Award Winning Australian Writing* (Melbourne Books, 2014)

'Of Coffee, Vegetables and Hair Colour' *The Sleepers Almanac* No. 7, 2011

'This Person Is Not That Person' *Award Winning Australian Writing* (Melbourne Books, 2014)

'Home Fires' *Famous Reporter* #44 (2012)

'Lost' *Award Winning Australian Writing* (Melbourne Books, 2010)

'The Gardener' *Escape* (Spineless Wonders, 2011); *Award Winning Australian Writing* (Melbourne Books, 2012)

'Fire Under the Skin' *Writing to the Edge* (Spineless Wonders, 2014)

'Night Shift' *Shibboleth and Other Stories* (Margaret River Press, 2016)

'Now, Voyager' *The Trouble with Flying and Other Stories* (Margaret River Press, 2014)

'Buoyancy' *Award Winning Australian Writing* (Melbourne Books, 2013, under the title 'Beyond Walls')

'Feather' *Page Seventeen* #6 2008 (under the title 'Rose')

Eight Seconds

All you need is eight seconds a day, said Gareth. Twice. Or three times.

What a deal! she said. At Tony Di Milia Flooring we have: Parquetry, Hardwood, Cypress Pine, Pelvic.

Gareth joined in the spirit of things. I'd like three centimetres of Pelvic Flooring, please.

As new, she said. Hard-wearing. Long-lasting.

Tongue and groove. Tight joins.

At Tony Di Milia we don't beat about the bush.

Slight imperfections are part of the charm.

Five babies, she said, suddenly sullen. What do you expect?

Gareth reached under the table and put his hand on her knee. I am so lucky.

His fish arrived a few seconds later.

She leant forward, wrinkled her nose. You never ask for fish at home. Funny, isn't it? Do you think we know all there is to know about each other? Without the children, who are we? She paused. Let's talk, then, about the things we'd like to fix in each other. I'll go first.

Gareth held the wedge of lemon over his plate and squeezed.

The way you scratch me, she said. I hate scratching. Well, not scratching as such, but pulling your fingernails along my skin. It's intensely irritating.

The way you gulp, said Gareth. Oh, my God. I hate that.

You have skinny eyes. Remember that movie? The kid said he has skinny eyes. They're not that skinny, by the way. But sometimes you have this blank look. Like you're not all there. Adrift. And you don't smile enough.

Your smile is not always genuine when you say hello to someone in the street. Why pretend you're pleased to see them?

Why just stand there with a blank look? It's rude.

Gareth separated a bone from the fish and placed it carefully on the side of his plate. Your wide hips, from the back, look like a giant soup tureen.

She took a loud gulp of champagne. Here's to us.

Cheers, he said, not disguising a grimace. After a moment, he spoke. There's a man at the bus stop in the morning who's very old. Maybe a hundred.

That's old.

Can you imagine being that old?

You mean me? Or us?

No one in particular. You.

So, I'm no one in particular?

You take offence too easily.

That comment was never on any of my report cards, she said. Straight As. Even for Attitude.

Up until then she'd only toyed with her eye fillet, but now she took the steak knife and swiftly hacked off a hunk and began to chew viciously.

The six translucent bones Gareth had eased from the fish lay in a neat row. He pushed the spinach puree to one side with his knife and skewered a baby potato.

I'm doing it here, now, she said, without looking at him.

Everything to your satisfaction? The waiter alongside in her black apron. Flat-bellied, slim-hipped.

What to say? No. It's awful. We're having a hideous time. My husband would like my vagina to be as tight as yours. I want him to smile more. I'm sitting here doing an eight-second pelvic floor exercise as I nod that everything's perfect, thank you.

After the waiter had left, Gareth reached into his jacket pocket and pulled out a small blue box bound with silver ribbon. With an expression that was loving, pinched and wary, he pushed the box across the table. Happy Anniversary.

Have you noticed how Robbie has been rolling his eyes? she said. Like this?

Gareth shook his head and glanced at the box. Maybe take him to the optometrist.

That's not what he needs. I think he's anxious.

Are you going to open it?

In a minute. Don't you think he might be anxious?

About what?

He's picking up on the atmosphere.

What atmosphere?

Would you care for dessert?

Could you give us a minute? said Gareth to the black apron. He leant forward and whispered, almost spat, Why don't you open it?

She looked away. Outside, through the vast window, the sky was a suffused rose on blue, and the moon, newly risen, shone foam white in contrast. She wondered whether it was full or whether there was the slightest shaving off its edge, and even as she wondered, she became aware of how dog-tired she felt.

She looked down at the box in front of her and heard Gareth urge her once more to open it. She did not want to open it. The question was, how could she come up with a reason not to?

She would give herself eight seconds.

The Uninvited

Perry ran across the oval. His trouser cuffs were wet, his bare feet numb. He had no idea where he was heading. Just knew he wanted to be far away. Maybe take a train to the airport. Fly to London to see his brother.

Up on the road he slowed to catch his breath beside a cottage. A boy in pyjamas playing on the porch scampered inside. Perry could just make out his small shadow pressed against the flywire.

He hurried on. London was mad, Canberra better. He could stay with his friend Phil, if he still lived there. He wondered if Ella would be out looking for him. Right now their decision to be car-less was lucky for him.

A woman jogged by pushing a pram, breathing hard as she took on the slope. Ella despised the way women puffed and grimaced, running behind their offspring. She said they were drawing attention to themselves and their babies. Perry knew, but would never say, that this was her grief talking.

He stooped to examine the soles of his feet. Large blisters were forming, painful and fluid-filled. He wouldn't get far without shoes. Too early for the shops to be open and he had to keep moving. For a moment he stood, undecided. Two schoolboys sniggered as they passed, and he overheard the word *dero*.

He thought of the cottage with the boy in pyjamas. Might be a pair of the dad's shoes on the porch. He limped back, just in time to see a woman strapping a baby into her car. As the car backed out, he could see the boy's bright eyes staring at him through the rear window.

Only one child-sized red gumboot. Perry spun around to check if anyone was watching. With any luck there'd be a spare key. He scouted round the back and soon discovered it under a loose board.

The house smelt of milk, soiled nappies and toast. In the main bedroom Perry found nothing but women's shoes. He slipped his feet into a pair of mauve slippers and padded down the hallway, relishing the sensation of fleece against his raw skin. He paused to peer at a photo on the wall – a group on a dive boat. That would be the boy's mother, looking cold but joyful.

He heard the rattle of a key in the front door. She must have forgotten something. He ducked into the boy's room and slid under the bed. Hopefully, she'd be gone in a flash.

'Mummy, what's wrong?' It was the boy. 'I want to go to the park.'

Perry heard retching from the bathroom. The baby crying. Toilet paper unravelling. The splash of water in a basin.

'Mummy's sick, Max, we can't go to the park today.'

The baby's cries were getting louder. The woman was in the room now, rummaging through the toy box, the boy alongside, tugging at her jeans. Perry pressed his back against the skirting board and held his breath.

'I have to feed Rose. You can play with Thomas the Tank.'

'I want to watch a DVD.'

'The DVD player is broken. Remember?'

The boy began to whine. Like a giant mosquito, Perry thought.

'I'll play with you after I've fed the baby,' said the woman, her tone tinged with despair. Now the baby was in Perry's line of sight, deposited on the bedroom rug as the mother raced back to the bathroom, the boy in pursuit.

From under the bed Perry listened to the misery of it all – the whining boy in the bathroom with the vomiting mother, the baby hungry and screaming, her tiny arms rigid with fury, face in a scarlet pucker. Perry slid out and gathered her up in his arms. He tiptoed past the bathroom and into the kitchen. He found a sipper cup by the sink and filled it with juice.

In the bathroom he tapped the boy on the shoulder. The boy jumped and went quiet.

'Thirsty?'

The boy nodded, wet-eyed, taking the juice cup.

The woman, kneeling over the toilet bowl, lifted her ashen face. 'Who the hell are you?'

Perry saw bubbles of sweat on her forehead.

'I'm the DVD repairman,' he said. 'The front door was open. Can I get you anything?'

Before she could answer, the woman turned to the bowl again, heaving.

Perry took the boy's hand. 'Come on,' he said. 'Let's find you a snack.'

With the baby on his hip and the boy alongside, he returned to the kitchen. He found crackers for the boy. Then he hunted around for formula and a bottle and deftly mixed up some milk. He warmed it in the microwave and popped the teat into the baby's mouth.

'Max!' the mother called. 'Come here.'

'No, I stay here.'

'It's alright,' Perry called back. 'He's alright.'

'I don't know who you are. You're not a repairman.' This time an empty retching noise was followed by a groan. 'I never phoned for one,' came a weak voice. 'What are you doing in my house?'

Poor woman, thought Perry. Something she ate, perhaps. He sat on the couch with the baby, who was content now, sucking greedily, eyes roving over his face. Max sat at his feet, tootling cars up and down his legs. The sound of running water. The hum of an electric toothbrush. Perry braced himself for her questions.

There she was, holding herself up in the doorframe.

'I want to know who you are and what you're doing here. Just need some water.'

Perry nodded. He patted the baby and she released a soggy burp. He glanced at the woman, who was making her way gingerly towards the kitchen, holding her belly.

'I only hope I'm not pregnant,' he overheard.

Perry took a moment to survey the room. A mismatched collection of 1950s chairs at the kitchen table, which was a green laminex. Toy boxes upended, spilling onto the rug. An iPad on the bookshelf. The couch he was sitting on had worn patches on the arms. It was an orange check.

'How did you get in?' she snapped. She was pale. The hand holding a glass of water was trembling.

'The spare key,' said Perry, jolted from his reverie.

'Well, you can get out now. Give me my baby.'

Max looked up. 'You can stay and play with me if you want.'

Perry handed the woman her baby and she nearly lost her balance.

'Here,' he said, helping her to the couch.

'I said get out.'

'I will,' said Perry, then paused. 'I wonder – would you be able to lend me a pair of your husband's shoes?'

'What?'

'I have no shoes, you see. I didn't mean to scare you.'

She shook her head, noticing her slippers on his feet for the first time.

'Complicated,' said Perry.

Max rolled back on the floor. 'You doesn't have shoes!'

'Max,' she said, sharply. Then she rubbed her forehead with a resigned sigh. 'My husband has plenty of old joggers.' With a curl of the lip she added, 'Joggers are his thing. The laundry is that way. You should find a smelly old pair in there.'

'They stink!' said Max, giggling.

The plastic tub in the laundry held five pairs of running shoes. Worth a couple of hundred each, thought Perry. He took the least worn pair. They were roomy, so he pulled the laces tight, then tested them out with a little jump.

'Find them?' she called.

'Found them!'

There was a basket of wet washing on the floor. She was in no state to be hanging it out. Should he? He'd already outstayed his welcome. Not that he'd been exactly welcomed.

'Back in a minute,' he called. 'Hanging out your washing.'

'*No!*'

Perry took the basket out to the yard. A grey cat blinked drowsily from a patch of sun on a timber seat. A plastic trike lay on its side. Half-hidden in the foot-long grass was a baby's rattle. Cactuses in dirty clay pots. Homely, but neglected. Perhaps he could mow the lawn for her. He smacked his forehead – what was he thinking? He had to get a move on. Rose's cries drifted from the house. The woman was probably settling her to sleep after the feed. He pegged up tiny singlets, all-in-ones, and the only man's garment – an old Mambo t-shirt, XXL. Ex-surfie?

Ella had declared Perry's shirts dull and conservative. She said she couldn't bear to look at him sometimes. Why couldn't he wear something different? One by one she'd taken his shirts from the wardrobe and flung them across the room. 'Dull. Dull. *Dull.*' Then she'd twisted the metal hangers so nothing could hang on them.

Perry was famished. No breakfast. Would it be unreasonable to ask for a slice of bread? He could offer to make her a sandwich. No, her stomach would be too delicate. He could make her a cup of tea and dry toast, or crackers. He pegged out the last of the little socks.

Back inside, the woman looked at him as if to say, Well? Are you leaving now?

'Thanks for the shoes,' he said. 'I really appreciate it. I'm Perry.'

'Okay,' she said, without warmth. 'Madeleine.'

'Those are my dad's shoes,' said Max.

'Yes.'

'Do you know where my dad is?'

'Max. Quiet.'

Perry shook his head.

'Mummy says he's lost.'

'I wish you'd go,' Madeleine said.

'Would you like a cup of tea?' and when she didn't answer, he said, 'I'll put the kettle on. You can make up your mind later.'

In the kitchen a Spiderman bowl lay in the sink. Toast crumbs on the bench. A half-cup of cold coffee. Perry plugged in the kettle.

Madeleine had fallen asleep. Max was hunched over the DVD player instructions.

'Do you understand those?' Perry whispered.

Max shook his head. 'I like looking where the lines go. They take my finger here. And here.'

'Maybe you'll be a TV technician when you're older.'

'Maybe,' the boy said, lightly, as though he didn't really care.

'What did you mean when you said your dad was lost?'

'That's what Mummy says. She says we have to be good and wait. He'll find his way home soon. It's probably because he's looking for a new job.'

'When did he get lost?'

Max shrugged. 'Two, five, maybe 21 days ago.'

The kettle was boiling. Perry leapt up. He saw Madeleine's eyes open.

'Milk? Sugar?' he asked.

'Neither.'

She reached for the mug and the pads of their fingers touched. After a sip she appeared to relax.

'Better?' he said.

She stiffened. 'You have no right to be here.'

'No. I should never have entered your home. I'm truly sorry.'

There was a whimper from the bedroom.

Madeleine's face fell. 'I don't believe it. I was hoping she'd have at least an hour.' She went to fetch the baby and sat back down.

'Never do what you expect, do they?' said Perry.

'You have kids?'

'Had. One.'

He'd not mentioned his daughter to a soul for almost a year.

Madeleine looked worn out. Her hair was pulled back into a loose knot. Perry noticed fine strands of grey.

'It was a Sunday,' he said, feeling his way.

She sipped her tea, watching him. Rose was playing with her necklace.

'It was a Sunday in spring. The rain had let up, so I took her for a walk. The world – the sky, the leaves – everything was fresh and clean. Sparkling.' He picked up one of Max's toy cars and rolled it across his palm. 'Have you noticed how many men are cycling the bike path these days? How fast they go? There's just no warning.'

Both mother and son were quiet.

'She spotted a blue wren,' he went on. 'This little bird flitting about on the wrong side of the path. There was no warning.'

He nosed the car towards Max's toes. The boy drew his foot back with a squeal.

'Two years old.' Perry offered his hand. 'Let me take your cup. I'll head off now.'

Madeleine held it out. 'Before you go,' she said, softer now, 'can you tell me – why no shoes?'

'It was Ella,' he said. 'My wife. She thought I was going to leave her, so she disposed of all my shoes during the night. Last night. No idea what she did with them.'

'Wow.'

'I know. We've had our troubles. Ever since—'

'Yes,' she said. 'I understand. So…were you? About to leave?'

'No. But that was the tipping point.'

'So now you *are* leaving.'

Perry rinsed her cup and upturned it onto the rack. 'No,' he said. 'I'm going home.' He moved back to the lounge room. 'I want you to know that break-ins are quite out of character for me.'

'Call it a touch of lunacy.'

'Yes, that was it. Lunacy.' He glanced out the window. 'Must be due for a full moon.' He looked down at Rose. 'She's delightful.'

'A handful.'

'I'll return the shoes in a day or two.'

'Keep them.'

Perry leant down to ruffle Max's hair. 'See ya, buddy.'

'I hope you feel better soon. And thanks,' he said to Madeleine.

'To you too.'

He raised his eyebrows.

In a low voice she said, 'The kids, the chores… Gets hard sometimes.'

He glanced at Max, and whispered, 'Lost?'

She shook her head.

'Don't lose hope,' he said.

Perry closed the door gently behind him. He bounced on his toes for a moment to test out the shoes. They felt good.

Trainee

Three boys – maybe 14, 15 years old – shove and poke each other in the checkout lane. One of them lobs a jumbo Coke and a packet of Maltesers onto the conveyor belt.

Andrew clumsily loops the plastic bag over the metal supports.

One of the boys peers at the badge pinned to Andrew's shirt.

'Ann…Drew,' says the boy. 'How long ya bin workin here, Ann?'

Andrew's neck flushes. 'Two weeks,' he says, scanning the goods, not looking up.

'Good job?'

'Pretty good.' Andrew unloops the bag and places it in the pick-up area. 'That's five-fifty, thank you.'

'Who's paying for this lot? Spano – your turn.'

'Gis a pack of Stuyvesant too, Ann,' says Spano.

'Sorry. I'm not allowed.'

When he opens the till, Andrew realises he's out of two-dollar coins. He signals Tracy on the next checkout. She doesn't notice, or maybe she ignores him.

'Excuse me, Tracy,' he calls, but she's busy greeting each customer with a smile. *How are you today? That's good. How are you today? That's good. Do you have a loyalty card?* She's so at ease, he thinks, scanning items, chatting, as though born to the work.

It was towards the end of school term that Andrew's mum had said, 'Put on some clean pants and a shirt and be at the supermarket at 4:30. You've got an interview.' She'd just met the manager, she told him. She'd been looking after his father in the nursing home. The two-week training period is almost over. Tracy has cruised through without a hitch. Confident and chatty, she wears thick eyeliner and chunky black shoes to match.

The Shift Manager appears beside Andrew bearing keys and a bag of change. Andrew moves aside to make room for her.

'Lucky I was on the lookout, Andrew.' She delivers several rolls of coins into his till. 'Next time, use the PA to call me. Can't be watching you all shift.' She bustles off, keys jangling from her waist.

'Hear that, Ann? Betcha'd like it if she *was* watchin.'

'Do you have a loyalty card?'

'Just gis the change, Ann.'

Andrew carefully counts the coins into Spano's rough palm. He's already mucked up the change once this shift. Bad luck it was his maths teacher. She seemed sympathetic as she showed him her palm: 'I gave you 50 dollars.'

He'll practise change-giving at home, Andrew decides, as the next customer unloads her items. It's a woman in a suit buying coffee, tampons and vermicelli noodles. Trainees are instructed to ask for a customer's loyalty card without fail. For some reason Andrew can't project these words clearly, so he needs to repeat them, often. He hauls the words from somewhere deep within and directs them towards a mixed bag of expressions – bored, irritated, confused.

'Oh, yes. I always forget,' says the woman, reaching into her purse. 'There you go.' She smiles at him.

Andrew scans the card and hands it back. His neck reddens again when he packs the box of tampons. Trainees are taught not to react to the goods people choose to buy. Condoms. Pregnancy tests. Swags of pizzas and ice-cream for fat people. No comment. It's none of your business. It's SafeMart's business.

A man with skin like biscuit crumbs lays out white bread, tea bags, razor blades and five cans of No Frills cat food. Andrew hooks up the man's eco-bag. Here is a cat owner, he thinks.

'How are you today?' Andrew asks in what he hopes is a clear, confident voice.

'Not bad, mate.' The man tosses his basket into the stack, and lumbers through as though he's in pain. He sighs. 'Not bad at all, mate.'

'Still raining outside?' asks Andrew. He needn't have said *outside*, he thinks.

'Settled in for a few days, I reckon, mate.'

Andrew scans the cans. 'Rain's good for ducks, but not so good for cats.' Not brilliant, he thinks, but not too awful.

'You're right there, son.'

'Do you have a loyalty card?'

The cat food reminds Andrew of his tenth birthday. First thing his mother said was not *happy birthday*, but that a magpie had dive-bombed his cat. With theatrical hands she described the way the cat tore round the yard, yowling, before flinging itself over the fence. This frightened, mangy cat Andrew had carried home in his school bag and nurtured back to health. The cat was never seen again. As he grew older, he often wondered whether the magpie story was the truth, whether his mum had let his cat loose on the world to fend for itself. She'd lost her job. She was broke. Cat-food expenses were adding up. Not only this, her nose was always running, her eyes watering.

'I'm allergic to cats,' she'd said.

Closing-time announcement has come and gone and it's nearly knock-off. Andrew wonders how to go about buying a Mars bar. He decides to get one at the hamburger place on the way to the bus stop, rather than bother the Shift Manager again. He hopes his mum has left dinner out for him before her night shift. It's his first payday tomorrow. After board, he hopes to have enough to buy *Eragon*, a book he's keen to read. And maybe he'll look for a low-maintenance, allergy-free pet.

As Andrew approaches the bus shelter he sees Spano in his hoodie. His arse tightens. He looks around to see if the other boys are nearby. Since seeing a TV program about what makes a victim a victim, Andrew's been practising in front of the mirror to not be one. Two burly bouncers on the show were supposed to be experts. It's all about body language, they said. Since this program, Andrew's been trying to walk upright and with purpose. He's not used to walking this way and it makes him feel weird. To avoid eye contact with Spano, he checks his watch. He looks in the direction the bus will come and shifts his daypack across his shoulders. The rain is heavier than ever.

It's not Spano. It's just a kid whose father is sitting in the shelter talking on his mobile. Andrew pulls himself up straight again, even swaggers.

There's no dinner for him, no note, so Andrew makes some toast. He slices some cheese, places it on the toast and scribbles tomato sauce over the top. He eats in the lounge room listening to John Coltrane – one of the old vinyls his dad left behind. He washes up, wipes down the kitchen bench, and goes to his mum's room, where he stands in front of the mirror and pulls his shoulders back.

'How are you today?' he says, with a smile. 'Do you have a loyalty card?'

Andrew reads for a while and falls asleep with the light on. He wakes in the early hours to his mum's key turning in the lock. He switches off his lamp and lies in the dark, thinking of the day ahead. The day has a two o'clock start time and a checkout lane reserved for him. And facing him on his bedside table sits a badge with his name on it.

Tripwire

The shot went off as Robin was studying the instructions on a box of couscous. She dropped to the floor. The corner of the box crumpled where it fell. It reminded Robin of a porcini mushroom.

He locked the door and flipped the sign to Closed. He kicked across a carton of soup cans as a barricade. The blood vessel in his neck made Robin think of a lizard on dry, red earth. The backs of his hands glistened.

The shop owner – 'Carmen' was the name on her badge – stood motionless at the register. In the opposite aisle a baby lay asleep in its pouch under the shelter of its mother's hands. If it woke and started crying it could tip the guy over, thought Robin. The only other customer was a boy in board shorts and skate shoes, about 18. He seemed disoriented as though he thought it might be a movie. His basket held a packet of Doritos, a big Coke bottle spangled with moisture and a pile of two-minute noodles. His mates would be hanging out for their breakfast.

Robin lowered her head onto her arms. She could smell her breath and its familiar odour of fear. Her gums were tacky. She tried slow-breathing to calm her heart.

Robin heard Carmen pleading. Mister, mister, please. Take what you want, mister. There's a baby here. Don't hurt anyone.

The mini-market was stocked with groceries, confectionary, fishing tackle and beach toys on high, skinny shelves. Robin usually drove to the cheaper supermarket in town, but today was all about suiting herself, which, one year on, still felt like a novelty.

The man pointed his gun first at one, then the other. The baby woke and began to gurgle, kicking its bare feet, making wriggly stars of its hands. The mother blinked in fear. The teenager stared at the floor. Robin wanted to catch his eye, to send him reassurance. His long legs with their coarse hairs were a man's and not quite a man's.

Nobody move. Everyone does the right thing, no one gets hurt.

He swung around, his back to the walls, like a TV cop.

Outside, an elderly couple stopped by the door. The man wore a bucket hat and carried an empty calico shopping bag. The woman's fine white hair looked newly trimmed. She made a remark and pointed to the Closed sign, but he shook his head. She gave his sleeve a tug and eventually he followed.

The baby started to cry. Robin peeked over her arms at the mother jiggling and patting.

Shut up. Shut up, the man said to the baby, to the mother.

In his eyes Robin recognised high alert. She'd seen it in her own in a darkened mirror as she waited for a footfall. Nerves taut as tripwire. She knew what it was like to tread an area lined with red and white rocks. The anticipation can destroy you.

The baby's cries grew louder. The mother rummaged desperately in the soft bag slung over her shoulder.

Shut the fuck up!

The teenager's hand crept to his pocket. Robin saw the outline of a phone. Don't even try, she thought. And yet if he could manage it without being seen… She needed to create a distraction.

The baby's hungry, she said to the gunman. He needs to eat.

The man swung around. Who told you to speak?

Robin's heart rabbited in her chest. She thought she caught the smell of him: aftershave, sweat, maleness. Such a smell used to linger in her bedroom. Their eyes locked. Instead of hunter, she saw hunted. It must have been the adrenaline rush that made her think of her class on word-play day: What vowel turns 'hunted' into a word meaning 'tormented by memories'?

This was to have been a good start to a good week. After stocking up on groceries she was planning to collect Molly from the holiday flat and take her to the dog park. Tire her out with ball-chasing then head to the beach for a swim. An afternoon movie at the heritage picture house. A healthy dinner. A good book. An ordinary yet most special of days, marking the anniversary of her leaving.

The boy had managed to extract his phone.

Sir, Carmen said, who'd also noticed, I have 500 dollars in here. And more out the back. Let me get it for you.

You take me for a fool? Do you?

No, sir.

The baby's cries grew louder. The man began marching up and down the narrow aisles, flinging items off the shelves. The mother wept silently. The boy took that moment to swipe his phone, seconds before the gunman rounded the corner. The man's hand shot out and the phone smacked into the ice-cream chest.

He thrust a jar of Heinz at the woman. Make him shut up.

Robin hoped the mother would ask him to take the lid off. She'd read that asking someone to do you a favour had the odd result of making them feel connected to you. The mother could even hand him the baby spoon she'd pulled from her bag.

They'd returned, the elderly pair. Others had passed, seen the sign, walked on, but these two were puzzled by the closure. The man's shopping bag now held a newspaper. He checked his watch and said something to the woman. He tried the door handle.

Don't move, said the gunman. Anyone moves and they get shot. So does the old man.

The woman shaded her eyes as she peered in.

Tell them you have refrigeration issues, he told Carmen. Closed all morning. He hid the gun behind his back.

Carmen made her way from behind the counter to the window where she waved, smiling stiffly.

Hurry up, said the gunman.

Sorry, we are closed, said Carmen. The fridges are not working.

The woman outside signalled a thankyou and beckoned the man, who was frowning. After a moment he joined her, and they walked on.

The 18-year-old's shoulders were shaking.

It'll be okay, Robin said to him.

Didn't I say shut up?

Robin thought if she got through this day and didn't die, how much would she remember? It was the waiting that frayed the nerves. She used to jolt awake in the mornings and within moments her mind and her pulse were racing. Adversaries could be anywhere. For anyone. Home or battlefield. She imagined the gunman scrambling out of his sleeping bag in a barren landscape, fully primed.

Couscous was perfect with vegetables, meat and fish, Robin read. It had a Facebook page. If she got out of here alive she would *like* it.

The baby was still crying. The mother's trembling hands couldn't get the lid off the jar.

The man had gone quiet. He was turning the gun over in his hand, examining it. Robin took the opportunity to study him. About 28, thick-set and fit, with close-cropped hair. No embellishments, no tattoos, only a silver chain necklace tucked under his t-shirt and a woven leather bracelet on his wrist.

All of a sudden he looked the teenage boy up and down. At your age I had my life mapped out, he said. Every last contour. Every last mountain.

River. Desert. Nothing I couldn't conquer. He looked down again at his gun. In a few seconds we could all be dead. It's that simple.

The boy reached into his basket for the Doritos. The crackling sound made Robin jump.

You must pay first, said Carmen.

You think this is a party? said the man. And for fuck's sake, shut that baby up!

Robin exchanged glances with the frantic mother. The baby's face was scarlet and wet with tears and mucus.

Listen, said Robin. How about I help with the baby?

The man looked at Robin. Robin held his gaze, feeling oddly calm.

No false moves, he said.

Robin stretched her cramped limbs and made her way over.

She smiled at the mother and took the jar of baby food. The lid was tight. She wiped her palm on her pants.

I was supposed to get married in this town. Next month.

They all looked at each other. Were they supposed to answer?

She doesn't want me now.

That's – Carmen hesitated – that's too bad.

I had to see why this place was so special. This peaceful haven where she used to spend her family holidays. You people need to wake up, he said, his voice getting louder. Do you have any idea what shit is happening in the world? Do you? He strode to the window and looked out. You've got your smug little mini-mart, your fancy bakeries, your coffee shops selling double soy skim latte shit topped with stupid scummy hearts. He turned and waved the gun at them. The whole white-bread deal. And as for you surfies with nothing to worry about but the next bloody wave...

The boy's neck went pink.

He shoved his gun into his belt and moved to the mother and child. He snatched the jar and spoon from Robin. He spooned the orange gloop into the baby's waiting mouth.

All eyes were on the feeding baby. Robin was close enough to touch the man's hand. They were all suspended in this peculiar moment of tenderness.

What are you even *doing* here? Robin said quietly. Why *us*?

Why not you? You looking for a rhyme and reason? There is none.

He put the jar and spoon on a shelf and moved away. For a long moment he stood contemplating the muzzle of the gun until Carmen piped up. Mister you don't do that in my shop. You need to do that outside.

You don't think I'm serious?

What's your name? Robin asked.

Don't go all cop show on me.

My name's Robin and this is Carmen, and the baby is?

Beau, the mother said.

And this young man is?

Lachlan.

And Beau's mother is?

Claire.

What makes you think you can play with us like we're nothing? We all have names. We all have our struggles and histories. What gives you the right? Robin paused. Because you have nightmares? Because your girl-friend couldn't handle your nightmares?

He took his eyes off the gun and let out a slow breath. It's Pete, he said.

Beau knocked the spoon off the shelf. He hung down as far as he could, pointing his chubby finger at the floor. Robin picked it up.

Why don't you and me go for a walk, Pete? We'll walk down the street like we're on holiday in this nice seaside town, where nothing out of the ordinary ever happens. You and me. This is what we've come for. Family time. She moved to the shop door. It's so warm and beautiful out here, she said.

They heard it then. A distant wail. Robin thought Pete might lose it and grab the baby, tossing him like a grenade. But instead he heaved aside the carton of soup cans and took off. She watched him cross the road and run past the elderly couple waiting at a safe distance. She saw him dodge street bins, lamps, café tables, a dog, as though he was in a jungle, always low to the ground, watchful, before disappearing in the direction of the beach.

When the police began to tape off the mini-market Robin said she needed the box of couscous. She told them it was lying on the floor in the pasta aisle. The corner of it looked like a porcini mushroom, she explained. The young officer asked what a porcini mushroom was. They wouldn't let her fetch the couscous. They wouldn't bring it to her either. No tampering with evidence. The officer was dismissive, as though Robin was obstructing a most important day. One of the most important to date in the officer's career, in this uneventful seaside town.

Companion Planting

It's half past four and already getting dark. Cars whoosh along the wet road. I've been dawdling in a café with a thick slice of buttery banana bread and two cappuccinos, and for the past few minutes have had my eyes fixed on an elderly couple over the road. They're standing in front of a bookshop display window. He's tall, white-haired and carries a brown umbrella. She's shorter, rounder, white-haired too. She wears a high-waisted skirt and the type of snug shoes you buy in a chemist. It's as though the surrounding space is reserved for them, moves when they move. His hand goes to guide her by the elbow now as they enter the bookshop. His movement is measured, sure, and the woman, in her comfortable shoes, a thin re-usable shopping bag dangling from her arm, is as graceful as a swan.

Grace – the element Stephen and I appear to be missing. You can't twist or shape yourself into loving. Some natures have affinity; others do not. It's like companion planting – tomatoes and basil, beetroot and lettuce. I'm not sure that Stephen and I are companion plants.

'Another coffee?' The waiter is wiping the table next to mine, in his other hand a small tower of glasses.

I shake my head. 'I'll pay now.'

I cross the road.

The bookshop is old-fashioned, a rarity, with its dark varnished timber, its yellowing labels – *Travel*, *War*, *Poetry*. The lighting reminds me of my grandmother's drawing room. The owner's head is buried in a book behind the high, dented and scratched counter. He nods a brief greeting.

'Happy to browse?' he asks. He takes a sip from a mug illustrated with a cartoon.

I nod, grateful not to have to talk.

I linger in *Travel*, leafing through the Lonely Planet guides, imagining I'm about to head off on an overseas trip. New backpack, walking shoes, passport. A tube of travel wash. A money belt. How do you take money overseas these days? I haven't travelled in 20 years. What I'd give to leave my life behind, board a plane, end up in some hilltop village where no one knows me.

I move to the counter. The man looks up.

'I saw an elderly couple come in not long ago. Have they left?'

'Oh, you must mean Don and Pam,' he says. 'They're here for Book Club. Are you a new member? It's upstairs.'

'Me? Oh, no. I was just wondering where they went.' I'm not a joiner. It's the old joke – I wouldn't want to belong to a club that would take me as a member.

'Friend of theirs?' he asks.

'Not really,' I say. I can't explain it – the way I've been watching them from the café, wondering how it's done, this finding a companion plant. How do some people so naturally settle into their soil together? How do they recognise each other?

I can see the cartoon on his coffee mug now: a bald-headed man pushing against a door that says *Pull*. The sign alongside reads: *Midvale School for the Gifted*. I smile.

'My son gave it to me for my birthday,' he says, holding it up. 'Not sure what he was trying to tell me.'

'That you have a sense of humour, I'd say.'

His head gleams under the light. My guess is he shaves what's left of his hair and makes up for it with a substantial moustache.

'Were you looking for anything in particular?'

'I'm not sure.'

'Apart from Don and Pam.'

'Sounds creepy.'

'Tell you what,' he says. 'Why don't you go upstairs and sit in on the book club? No one will mind.'

'Well...' I glance at my watch. 'It's almost five o'clock.'

'You have somewhere to be.'

I did, but while I was in the café wondering if I had the courage to bring up the subject of a separation, it was the thought of Stephen's possible reactions – contempt, anger or cold indifference – that made me want to delay going home. But Sean gets dropped off at six. I make him a hot Milo as he pulls off his boots and perches flushed and sweaty on the kitchen stool to tell me all about soccer training. Life as my son has known it for 12 years might be turned inside out. My eyes sting.

All this is passing through my mind as I stand at a bookshop counter in front of this bald, kind man who is studying me through wire-framed glasses. I get the peculiar feeling that if I tell him everything he'll understand. I won't, of course. I'm not the type to blurt out personal problems.

'I might go up for a few minutes.'

He guides me up a narrow flight of carpeted stairs. I hear the murmur of voices as we near the top. To the enquiring faces turned in my direction he introduces me as 'someone who's interested in joining'. I sit down and smile a brief hello.

'Don't let me interrupt.'

They're discussing *The Secret River*. A woman with plaits is saying that she found it hard-going. The man next to her, in a suit and tie, responds by saying the story gripped him from the start. Pam and Don sit quietly side by side on a small, brown velour couch. Behind them the light from the street slants through the window, and rain splatters the pane. It's cosy in this room with these unknown people.

Next to me is a woman in a lumpy green jumper who appears to be in charge. She wears bright red lipstick and has almond-shaped hazel eyes and a face that radiates. I've often wished my face radiated. Instead, mine is spiky, sombre.

'How did you find the descriptions of life on the Thames, Don?' she asks.

'Very accurate,' says Don, in a soft British accent. 'For the river, I mean. I'm no expert on the living conditions. So harsh, in those days.'

Pam seems restless. She stands, but Don gently tugs her fingers, pulling her to sit.

'I have to go,' she says, getting up again. 'I have to mark the papers, you see.' Don places his hand on her arm. Pam shakes it off, saying, 'Let me go! Don't you see it's time to review the information?'

'Right, everyone,' says the woman in the green jumper, clapping her hands. 'The kettle's boiled. I think it's time for a break, don't you?'

They all agree. Don, looking distressed, apologises, but the group is understanding. He moves to the narrow table set with a kettle and two plates of Arnott's assorted biscuits and some cups. I watch his knobby fingers dip a teabag in and out of a cup of hot water, all the while keeping a weather eye on Pam, who has wandered to the stairs leading to the bookshop below. She calls out in a loud voice, 'Hello, do I know you?'

'Yes, Mum, it's me, Phillip.'

The bookshop owner appears and leads Pam back into the room. Pam settles in under his arm and rests her head on his shoulder.

'You seem to be a very nice person,' she says.

'Come over here for your tea, Mum.' Phillip guides Pam to a chair by the window, pulls up a stool and sits next to her.

Don hands Pam her tea and stands nearby. I study the three of them.

Here, now, is affinity. Even though Don and Pam might bend in this final squall in their long partnership, they won't break. And Phillip – well, it's clear he comes from the same garden.

I'm finally beginning to accept that Stephen and I do not have what it takes to go the distance. I can't see either of us caring for the other with such selfless kindness into old age. And what about Sean? Would he be impatient or bitter towards us?

I notice Phillip's gaze on me. Perhaps he recognises a troubled mind. My worries pale in the face of his, however.

'Mum used to be an English teacher,' he says, moving towards me. 'We thought it'd be a good idea to bring her here. Familiar environment, discussing literature.'

'Of course,' I say. 'Great idea. And the bookshop might remind her of a library.'

'Exactly. Are you a reader?'

'Yes, only not so much lately.'

'Well, book club meets first Tuesday of the month. Lou will look after you.' He nods towards the woman in the green jumper, who's beginning to round everyone up.

It's really getting late now. I have to go. I have an impulse to speak to Pam, to say goodbye. Her eyes are so blue and clear I can hardly believe her mind is cloudy. She squeezes my hand.

'The results will be in soon,' she says. 'I'm sure you'll do well.'

I realise she's in a high-school classroom with a student, but I choose to take those words with me and hold them close.

'Join us next month,' says Don. 'We're reading *A Fortunate Life*.'

Phillip leads the way down the stairs to unlock the door. 'Well, you found your old couple,' he says. 'Not quite what you imagined?'

'You didn't tell me they were your parents! They are so much *more* than I imagined. How long have they been married? Forty, 50 years?'

'Don and Pam?' he says, a spark of mischief in his eyes. 'Married five years ago on the headland by the lighthouse.'

'What?'

'My father died a decade ago. Mum met Don at the orchid society.'

'You trickster.'

'I told not a single fib.'

'But I could swear they've been together forever.'

Phillip stands there, with his arms folded against the cold, smiling. 'There you go. That's people for you.'

'Hmm.' A gust of wet wind whips up the street. I pull on my beanie and loop my scarf around my neck. 'I'd better go. It's been really nice.'

'See you next month?'

I raise my eyebrows. 'The results will be in soon.'

Angie's Sparkle

The first time I met Verity Plummer in her smart heels I knew she wouldn't tolerate ineptitude.

'Do my desk, but don't disturb the papers. Toilet roll *down* from the top, not *up* from the bottom. Don't feed the cats.'

I'd advertised my services in a letter-box drop: *Don't sweat the small stuff. Reliable cleaner. Reasonable rates.* To date I have three clients: Verity Plummer, lawyer, two white cats (Boris and Mitzi); Tom Stanley, recently divorced builder; Gwen Glover, widow in her 70s whose daughter presented me as a six-month gift voucher. All three have agreed to Tuesday, once a fortnight.

I clear the breakfast table and gather up my cleaning gear.

'I'll come with you,' says Fran, my sister, gulping the dregs of her tea. 'Give you a hand.'

'I've been placed in a position of trust,' I say. 'You know – their keys, their houses?'

'What am I going to do – spill Handy Andy on the shag pile?' Fran pushes her chair back with a loud scrape. 'I'd like to help.'

My sister is big. Big laugh, big bust. Her voice enters a room before she does. She's the sort of person who doesn't hesitate to send back lukewarm coffee. Me, I don't mind lukewarm coffee. I'm just grateful to be served.

Fran and I rarely visit each other. Our relationship subsists instead on the occasional dutiful phone call. Yet two days ago she landed on my doorstep from Melbourne. She tells me she has a job selling women's plus-sized business clothing and the shop is undergoing renovations, so she had the brainwave to visit her little sister. I'm apprehensive about spending time with Fran, especially in these early days of my business. I need a clear head.

I consent to her coming with me on the condition she does things my way. I put on my white cap, grab the bundle of keys and a clean, dry mop and head out to the van. Fran follows, taking a final drag on her cigarette. When she stubs it out before climbing in I raise my eyebrows. Small changes. Once upon a time she'd have smoked in the car.

The aloof Boris skitters under a chair when I open the door. A purring Mitzi twines round my ankles. The creamy furnishings of this spacious apartment suggest independence and a high salary. I'd place Verity Plummer in her late 30s, a few years younger than me. Fran heads off on a self-guided tour, while I start dusting the lounge room. Verity appears to have entertained romantic company last night – two brandy glasses on the coffee table and a Portishead CD on the hearthrug.

It's been almost three years since my last intimate encounter. After our shop failed, Brian and I came to the blinding conclusion we had little in common. The daily hope that we would wake up and say something nice to each other, or even have some fun, had worn us out and a year later we divorced. I walked past the shop the other day. The new owners have installed stylish metal stools and a green awning. The words *Trans Fat Free* now feature on the signs. This might have saved our business. We were behind the times.

Brian and the new woman moved to the Sunshine Coast and opened up an organic coffee/Balinese knick-knack shop. He was considerate enough to send me a photo of the two of them aglow in the shop doorway. She's leaning into his turquoise-and-pink hibiscus shirt, dressed in a white, off-the-shoulder bit of skimpiness. You can almost smell the coconut oil gleaming on his greying chest hairs. He's travelling sweet and I have a couple of sour spots, but in truth I'm relieved.

As I'm sweeping the kitchen floor, Fran calls from Verity's study, 'Get a load of this.'

'What?'

'Receipt from Prouds. Two thousand bucks. A diamond ring.'

'Stop nosing about.'

'Do you suppose she bought it herself?'

'Why not? She has a good job.'

'It's like buying yourself an engagement ring.'

I refrain from comment, having just washed lipstick off both brandy glasses. Client loyalty prevents me from revealing her secret.

Before leaving, I pocket the envelope propped against the ice-blue retro kettle. *Angela* is penned across it in a flourish of curlicues. My clients and I rarely speak face to face, but they manage to communicate via their distinctive handwriting, via their belongings, and the surfaces I polish. They've kick-started my business and given me permission to enter their homes, bringing me closer to my dream of having 'Angie's Sparkle' professionally painted on the side of my van.

On the way to Tom Stanley's, Fran asks if I've been lonely since Brian left. I look at her suspiciously. Talking about feelings is unfamiliar territory for us, but she seems genuinely interested.

'I'm fine with it,' I say. 'I'm happy. How about you? Seeing anyone?'

'I was,' she says. 'I liked him, but it didn't work out.' She runs her finger across the dashboard. 'That was a few years back.' She belts out a laugh. 'Don't get me wrong – I've had my fair share of shags since then.'

It's a relief when the sight of Tom's townhouse brings the conversation to an end. She's my sister, but her bolshie manner can grate. I remember the day she stepped up to the front door to 'interview' my alarmed boyfriend, all of 17, and proceeded to shove a condom in my purse and a packet of cigarettes at him. I was so mortified I hardly spoke until we got to the cinema.

When I first met Tom to talk over the cleaning arrangements, my eyes were drawn instantly to the sock-height bands of white, almost hairless, skin above his thonged feet. Further up, the grey hide of his knees seemed a reflection of his home – softness under a tough masculinity. I saw remnants of the children he had on weekends – footy cards, DVDs, Macca's toys and sports socks. Things untended. I imagined Tom strumming the old guitar on the couch at night to keep the ghosts at bay. The framed photo of his boys on the cabinet was several years out of date.

'Good-looking boys,' says Fran, picking it up. 'What's the dad like?'

I'm dusting the bookshelf with its collection of model vintage cars. 'Nice enough, I suppose.'

'I mean is he a good sort?'

'Haven't given it much thought.'

'Oh, Ange,' Fran says, throwing her hands in the air, 'don't you ever want to have sex again?'

'Too busy.' I cross the room to put the photo back in place. After a pause, despite myself, I say, 'Apparently the divorce came through a few months ago.'

'Wonder if he's started dating.' Fran peers into his bedroom. 'Hmm, guess not. Not with this choice pile of jocks.'

Later, when I'm wiping the kitchen bench, I notice an open letter. I scan it and wish I hadn't. It's Tom's dad asking for money. I have no desire to get involved with my clients' lives. I have a business to run, and getting involved can take your eye off your goal.

Some days I open the phone book to read down the names until I find mine, and think, that's all we are, names on a list. Next year they'll have new names. Some will have dropped off. What sets each of us apart? The occasional bold font for a business. Next year I hope to see **Angie's Sparkle** listed in bold. I will be given more keys, invited into more homes.

We arrive at Gwen Glover's to see an ambulance in the driveway. The front door of the tiny honey-brick home opens and her daughter, Tillie, appears with an overnight bag. Behind her is a stretcher suspended between two paramedics in blue. Down one end of the stretcher is Gwen's silvery hair; down the other, her white bowls shoes. Tuesday is bowls day. I leap out of the van.

'Hello, dear.' Gwen turns her pale face towards me. 'I felt tired this morning. I woke up tired.'

'They think it might be pneumonia,' says Tillie. 'She was shivering all night.'

Fran comes over and pats Gwen's hand, murmuring an introduction. Gwen smiles up at her. Gentleness – here's another subtle change I've observed in my sister.

I turn to Tillie and in a low voice ask, 'Should I go, or would you still like me to clean?'

'Please stay,' she says, 'for today. I'll have to let you know about next time.'

Hanging between us is the implication of these instructions.

'Mum's very grateful,' Tillie says. 'The house has never looked so shiny.'

As the ambulance pulls out, Fran and I take the cleaning gear inside. Outside the kitchen window the wide cups of a blooming magnolia tree look set to hold wine at a wedding. On the sill is a dried chicken wishbone. As always, Gwen has laid out refreshments – a mug with a spoonful of instant coffee in the bottom, and two Honey Jumbles on a saucer.

As I take the bulging garbage bag from under the kitchen sink I notice a bloodstained tissue on the floor. Fran picks it up and we look at each other. 'Remind you of something?' she says.

Thrusting the memory aside, I tie a knot in the bag and move to the lounge room with my feather duster. Gwen collects green. Green plates, green vases, green china frogs. They all sit on shelves, making dusting tricky.

As she's shaking out the breakfast cloth, Fran says, 'I found a lump a few weeks ago.'

My blood shoots south. I collapse into Gwen's armchair.

'It's okay. I had a biopsy. It's benign.'

I pick at the cobwebs on the duster.

'It's not your fault,' she says.

'What a sister I am.'

'Ditto. I'm as much to blame.'

Fran takes the duster from my hand and nudges it across the bookshelf. 'You realise Mum would have been Gwen's age by now.'

I nod.

'Ever think about that day?'

'Try not to.'

'I have been lately.'

I press my toe to the vacuum cleaner, hoping the noise will silence my thoughts, but they're hurtling back. Blood on the kitchen floor. Broken glass from a vodka bottle. Ambulance siren. Me kneeling with tissues. My sister pulling me away, pulling my face to her chest. My big, loving sister. A long time ago.

Time. It's only a matter of time before Fran returns to Melbourne and all I've done for her is take her on my cleaning rounds. I'm waiting for the time when I've earned enough money for a permanent ad in the local paper, and maybe a fleet of subcontractor vans sporting a fancy sign. Is this the last time I clean for Gwen?

Fran takes the vase of wilted freesias from the coffee table. 'I noticed these growing by the front step. I'll pick some fresh ones.'

She returns with a yellow handful and holds them under my nose.

'So sweet,' I say, breathing deeply.

'Let's visit Gwen in hospital,' says Fran. 'We can take her a bunch.'

The laughing starts when we're in my kitchen peeling and chopping for stir-fry. We're remembering Fran's 16th-birthday dinner. After we'd managed to not choke on her hideous sloppy quiches, Mum then lurched back to the kitchen, returning with two frozen Apricot Danishes. The knife was useless, so she began attacking the Danishes with a hammer and chisel and ended up crying under the table nursing a bruised thumb.

Wiping her eyes, Fran says, 'I always admired you. The way you just got on with things, never erupting. Never losing it.'

I sweep the chopped onions into the wok. 'I looked up to *you*. I always wished I had your confidence. Your fight.'

'It's all a big fat front.' Fran points at her chest. 'Literally!' And we're off again.

We stand shoulder to shoulder at the bench. The words continue to flow. One subject we have no need to discuss is the absence of children. That much between us is understood.

After dinner we sit on the porch. I tell Fran about my plans for the house, once the money comes in. Timber decking will replace the old flagstone. I'll buy a new front door. A lemon tree. Brian's old study will get a lick of paint and some curtains.

'Make a great bedroom,' I say.

'Mmm,' she says. 'Yes, it would.'

We sit in easy silence. The evening air is tinged with a hint of the coming spring. Spring-cleaning. Now, there's a possibility. Grime on windows, venetians grey with dust, bathroom ceilings specked with mould. People will be on the lookout for a reliable cleaner with reasonable rates. Things are looking bright.

Of Coffee, Vegetables and Hair Colour

It's an afternoon in early summer and I've been sweeping the back porch listening to Mr Santis croon Greek lullabies as he works his garden. When the singing stops I look up to see his face at the fence.

'Can you please help with tomatoes?' He holds his hands up with an apologetic shrug. 'Arthritis.'

I put down my broom and go round to his garden. We loop his tomato plants to stakes with soft twine. Mr Santis also grows capsicums, and egg-plants the size of torpedoes. When he tells me his wife, Anna, has been dead for two years I am embarrassed not to have known.

Since then, I've learnt to pinch out the high laterals. I also weed, and pour tea-coloured worm water onto the plants. On the days Sam's not at preschool he comes too. A kind of peace descends on my son when we're in that fruitful yard.

One day Mr Santis surprises me with a request to help him colour his hair. It isn't easy for him to reach the back of his head, he tells me, and rinsing is equally troublesome.

With gloved fingers I tentatively work the blue-black dye into his loose scalp as he leans over the bathroom basin. 'Special occasion?' I ask.

'Sixty-five.'

'Today?'

'In a coupla months. Adonis I am not. But neither am I dead.'

My own faded hair reproaches me in the mirror as I wipe colour from Mr Santis's neck and ears with cotton wool. The ancient Saxons used to dye their hair before going into battle. For me – too late.

I don't discuss my visits next door with Garry, but one day when Sam is plucking the first cherry tomatoes, I happen to glance up at our house, smiling, to see that my husband is home early. His face looking down from our bedroom window is grim and grey, and I deflate in an instant. Our smiles are no longer for each other.

Mr Santis's hair needs tending to every four or five weeks and we establish a routine. He places a packet of Clairol on the birdfeeder hanging from his lemon tree. The birdfeeder is in my line of sight from the kitchen window. By now Mr Santis is familiar with Sam's preschool schedule, so the packet-placing always falls on a Sam-free day.

I pop over round 10.

'The roots is showing.'

'They are, Mr Santis.'

In the hallway the framed Anna has the glamour of a European film star, with a glossy tumble of dark hair. The kitchen smells richly of coffee. On the small, square table, a blue ceramic bowl gleams with tomatoes. A slice of feta sits on a saucer. The radio is tuned to easy listening.

I'm not exactly a fan of Mr Santis's new hair colour. The skin on his face is pliable and smooth, like walnut-coloured plasticine. Natural grey or silver hair would look striking.

'What made you decide on black?' I ask, wrapping his hair in cling wrap.

'I'm tired of looking old.'

We move back to the kitchen to wait for the colour to take. Sunlight highlights the slightly grimy seams of the stove. A briki sits on one of the hotplates.

'You don't look old,' I say. 'Your face is lived in.'

'Perhaps it's my life. It is old. Dull.'

'Your children?' I ask, hesitantly. 'Your garden?'

'These are things, yes. They bring some life.'

He stirs a coffee for me. A small white cup, not much bigger than an eggcup, brimful with liquid – thick, dark and sweet. I say nothing more about his hair. I check my watch. 'Twenty minutes is up.'

The back of his neck above his singlet is tawny, sprouting short, wiry hairs. Below, his back is pale, muscular. Black dye swirls down the plughole.

As I hand him the towel my mobile rings. Sam has vomited at preschool.

Mr Santis drapes the towel round his shoulders. His newly black hair is damp and tangled. He pats my hand. 'You go. You go get Sam.'

In the rear-view mirror Sam's pale face rests on the booster's wing. I stop at the chemist for some Children's Panadol. When we get home, I run a bath. He hasn't vomited again, but his clothes smell. I tip in a double dose of bubble bath, and once he's settled in the water I perch on the toilet seat. He tells me all about his vomiting episode. It happened after morning tea. He did it in the playground corner, on the concrete. Not on any toys.

'That's lucky.'

'Yup.' He squeezes water from the penguin into his mouth. I see flecks of mould in the stream.

'Don't, Sammy. It's dirty.'

'I'm not swallowing.'

'You wouldn't want to vomit again.'

'I'm not going to. Can we go to Mr Santa's garden?'

'I think you should have a nap.'

'No. *No* nap.'

'After your nap we'll go.'

He fiddles with his penis under the bubbles.

'Sometimes I don't like you,' he says. He takes the penguin and plunges it headfirst into the water. 'Or Daddy.'

'I don't think you mean that.'

'How was your day?'

Garry's had a shower, changed into shorts and a t-shirt, and is on the floor watching Sam with his *Bob the Builder* toys. The question doesn't seem directed at me, so I don't answer.

'Still not talking?' His tone is sarcastic.

'Oh. You mean me? Okay. My day. Helped Mr Santis with his hair. Picked up our son after he threw up at preschool. Bathed him. Took care of him for the rest of the day. Not as productive as your day, no doubt.'

'I reckon he gets a kick out of it.'

'Who? What?'

'The old guy. Santis.'

'Hardly.'

'Ever groped you? Stuck his hand up your skirt?'

'I'm not even going to answer that.'

'Mr Santa gives me 'matoes,' says Sam. 'He's nice to me and Mummy.'

We have days and days of rain. It thuds onto the roof like a thousand leather boots. Sam and I dash into preschool, panting. At home I watch water cascade over the edge of the clogged gutters. I miss Mr Santis's garden.

When the rain lets up, I wade through the dirty water in the laundry, my toes pearly white like a child's. I scoop into the blocked veins of our house. The sludge of debris, the gum tree's limp leaves.

Outside, the towels hang straight and heavy. Beneath the clothesline, Sam is poking a muesli bar into the rabbit hutch.

'No, Sammy. It's not rabbit food.'

He takes a bite himself. What diseases can be passed from a rabbit to a four-year-old? I feel I don't know enough. About anything. I can't tell my child *stuff.*

A mist has descended. Garry phones. There's a line of cars end to end along the highway to our home. He'll be late. I rejoice.

We are hazard lights, blinking in the fog.

'Today we play Big School. We practise Big School.'

'What did you practise?'

'Lining up. Bell ringing. Teachers.'

'Fun?'

'Mmm.'

From his booster seat, Sam's eyes follow the passing scenery. I'd dropped out of teacher training after I lost the baby, when Sam was two, because I couldn't drag my intellect out of the murky landscape of pain. I'd planned to go back when Sam started school, but now I feel a surge of panic at the thought. My son is primed for the next phase of his life, but I am floundering. If only all I needed to worry about was where to go at lunchtime and how to make friends.

Garry and I spend an entire Sunday not speaking. Sam becomes a means of highlighting our carelessness of each other. The more we laugh and play with him, separately, the more conspicuous our cold silences.

The rain returns, relentless. Small leaks are sprouting, trickling down walls. I roll up old towels and stuff them against skirting boards. The house is full of holes. I take forensic pleasure in plugging the holes of our house.

Weeks pass without the Clairol packet appearing on the birdfeeder. By early autumn I notice that Mr Santis's tomato plants have withered, hanging brown and forlorn, with only a few remaining fruit. I decide to offer to help him pull them up. Sam knocks on the door for me. After a couple of minutes, it opens. Mr Santis is unshaven, with an inch of grey roots down his part.

'Come in.'

'Are we disturbing you?'

'I am doing nothing,' he says.

We follow him into the kitchen, where he sits heavily on a chair. I see signs of neglect. Dishes. Mouldy oranges. A posse of flies zigzags beneath the light above the table.

'We thought we'd help with your tomato plants.'

'I give up the garden.'

'Oh, no.'

'No one eat it. Autumn comes. I have no winter seedlings ready.'

'And your hair?'

'Forget it. I look stupid. It is stupid.'

Sam has been hanging behind me, uncertain. He wanders out to the garden. 'Can I make you a coffee?' I ask Mr Santis.

'If you wish.'

'You'll have to teach me how to make Greek coffee.' I take the briki off the stove and rinse it.

He pulls himself up from the chair. 'There are three different types,' he says, opening a jar. '*Glyko* is sweet. Very sweet. *Metrio* is medium. And *sketo* is no sugar.'

'Which one do you usually make?'

'*Glyko*.'

He shows me how much coffee and sugar to put in the briki and I place it on the stove.

'You have to watch. It can be very quick.'

Just as the coffee is frothing to the lip of the briki I take it off. We sit at the table. 'Delicious.'

'You make it good for first time.'

'Ah. You smiled!'

'It's my daughter,' he tells me with a sigh. 'She's getting a divorce.'

'That's no good.'

'Of course it's no good!' His palm strikes the table. 'She has two boys. What will happen? The house breaks.'

'What went wrong?'

'She says she doesn't love him. *Agapi*. It changes. No one understand that these days.'

Garry receives a letter from his father. After 40 years his parents have decided to separate. The letter is a wad in Garry's fist as he swears at the floor.

'Not in front of Sam,' I say.

Garry looks at me, gets to his feet and is gone. I hear his car take off down the road.

'Where's Daddy going?'

'To get a newspaper I think.'

Garry doesn't return until bath-time. I glance up at him from my perch on the toilet seat. His crumpled face turns from me to Sam. He kneels by the bath. He takes the shark and manoeuvres it underwater to the *Jaws* theme until it's heading up the channel between Sam's legs. Sam squeals in terror-delight.

Later, in bed, we wordlessly make love.

Over the next few days Sam hits a recalcitrant patch, baulking at all requests. I lose my temper with him in the backyard when he refuses to put on his shoes, ruining his new socks in the mud. Mr Santis opens his back door, drawn out by my shouting. I'm mortified to think he has heard. He comes to the fence.

'I have decided to prepare my soil,' he says. 'Sam. Put on your shoes and come and help me. Bring Mama.'

We dig up weeds, and vegetables gone to seed. We turn over soil and uncover fat worms. Sam is introduced to olives and feta for afternoon tea. Mr Santis spreads chook pellets and compost over the soil. There's an aroma of earth and goodness. Rich, basic, warm. We're still in the garden when Garry arrives home and the lights go on in the house.

'We'd better go home, Sammy.'

'Call your husband. Ask him here. We will have *krasi*.'

I hesitate. It has been such a good day.

'Call your husband,' Mr Santis repeats.

I can see Garry at the kitchen window. I go to the fence and motion him with a wave. 'We're going to have some Greek wine. Come on over.'

After a few minutes Garry appears at the gate, uncertain. Sam hurtles into his legs. 'Daddy! Just look at all our work.'

As the sun sets on our glasses of wine, Mr Santis shows us Anna's sketches.

'She was very good. Look at this one.' It's a boy on a beach, a necklace of seaweed dangling from his hand. 'Look at the fingers. Perfect.'

I turn it over. *George Santis, 1974.*

'Our son,' says Mr Santis. 'He dead at 22. From accident at work.'

My womb tightens in shock.

The neighbourhood is moist and fragrant as we turn the corner to home, Sam asleep against Garry's chest. I hear the faint tinkle of cutlery.

A baby's lamb-like cry.

In bed that night I inch my way towards the centre and hold my breath. Garry's back is turned to me. A shaft of moonlight rests on his shoulder. I dip my hand into it. So pale. My ring gleams. My hand travels down the moonbeam until it alights on Garry's skin.

'Dad would like to visit,' his back says. 'I said I'd check with you.'

'That would be fine. Absolutely fine with me.'

By the next afternoon the last of the garden beds have been prepared. Sam is washing his hands under the tap. Mr Santis and I are standing back admiring the results of our labour when Garry appears at the gate with a box.

'Daddy!'

'I have zucchini,' Garry says. 'Spinach. Broad beans.'

My jaw drops. I peer into the box, touching each seedling in turn.

'The nursery gave me the scoop on winter vegetables.'

Mr Santis's eyes glisten as he takes the box. He grips Garry's arm. '*Efharisto*. Thank you.'

As the shadows lengthen, we plant. Mr Santis draws long furrows with a stick. Garry and I settle the seedlings into the soil. Sam's job is to water them in.

Later, in Mr Santis's kitchen, Garry sets to work gluing a corner of uplifted lino. The dishes are done, the table clean. Sam is racing his Matchbox car down the corridor.

'Any news of your daughter?' I ask Mr Santis.

'She's coming with her boys. For Easter.'

'Wonderful.'

'We will have lamb,' he says. 'Traditional Greek Easter. Sam will come to paint eggs with the boys.'

I glance at Garry.

'You will all join us to eat,' continues Mr Santis. A statement, rather than an invitation.

'Let us know what we can bring,' says Garry.

'I have one request,' Mr Santis says, turning to me. 'Can you help with hair colour before they arrive?'

This Person Is Not
That Person

Daniel leapt down the dunes, keeping his eye on the square of yellow light and Layla, inside. Anticipation ignited him.

The cabin door opened with the warm scent of her – paint, turps, musky talcum.

'I thought I told you not to come tonight,' she said.

Daniel hooked a finger into the waist of her drawstring pants and pulled himself to her. 'You can't keep me a secret forever.'

Layla glanced at her watch and turned to go in. 'Since you're here, you can make yourself useful and chop the vegetables.'

Daniel's hands trembled as he sliced the carrot into discs. Nights in this cabin with Layla were all he could think about. It was here he felt wanted. He'd started skipping school to spy on her as she painted. What difference did it make? Fucked-up school and fucked-up teachers, like every school he'd been to. They wouldn't care if they never saw him again. His dad wouldn't either.

'I want to see you more often,' he said, his heart pounding. 'Can't I come to your real home?'

'Not negotiable,' said Layla. 'This person is not that person.'

Daniel wiped his hands on the tea towel, and without looking at her asked, 'You having visitors?'

'I said no questions.' She closed the oven door.

Daniel's scalp pricked with sweat and his lungs contracted like fists. 'Another man?'

'Another man?' Layla laughed. She took a mandarin from the fruit bowl. 'Is that how you see yourself? As a *man*?' She stood, one hand on a hip, the other lightly juggling the mandarin. Her hands were tanned and smooth, nails cut straight and short.

Daniel felt the blood surge up his neck and into his cheeks. He couldn't take his eyes off the fruit. Up, down, up, down.

'Look,' she said, splitting the mandarin in two with her thumbs, 'it's as though I'm my own twin. Monozygotic. *Identical halves*,' she explained. 'This half is the only half you'll ever meet. Take it or leave it.' The halves dropped to the bench. Layla took off her top. 'Now get into bed like a good boy. We have 15 minutes.'

Daniel allowed her to lead him to the bedroom. A sudden wind had kicked up, whistling through the she-oaks and flinging itself at the cabin's flimsy joints.

The smell of the roast, the white walls, the thin floor, the small room. The pile of erotic drawings in the corner. A bottle of turps.

Afterwards, he lay watching Layla fasten her bra. He fingered the shells on the nightstand, the pebbles and bits of twine. There were bowls and jars of these throughout the cabin.

Layla tossed him his t-shirt.

'Could you stir the gravy?' she said. 'Just popping out to phone him. Cabin's out of range. Then you have to go.' She jabbed her thumb over her shoulder, in the direction of the door.

In the kitchen Daniel turned up the heat under the pan and gave it a stir. Then he went back to the bedroom. He held Layla's nightshirt to his face and inhaled before flinging it across the room. *Him.*

At first it was only the stainless-steel kettle flickering orange. Next came the thwump of flames up into the rangehood, bright and fierce, and the snap and blister of white paint.

Layla raced back into the cabin, yelling.

Years later, Daniel wondered whether he was trying to melt her down, the two halves of her, so he could take her away in a jar to keep on his nightstand. A reduction of paint and shells that he could hold up to the light forever.

Down Came a Blackbird

It was early evening when I crunched down the path to my sister's house, a weatherboard on the edge of a bushland valley. The door opened, and Toby nearly knocked me down with a fierce hug.

'What's that?' He pointed to my paper bag.

'A bottle of wine.'

'Are you going to get drunk?'

'No!' I laughed, a little disconcerted.

Jayne had phoned me in the morning pleading a migraine, but I told her I was still coming, it was all arranged, right down to the dog-minder. In any case, I hadn't seen Toby for almost two years — not from want of trying. I'd accepted her excuses every time, but recently I'd become concerned at her blurry late-night calls. She'd lapse into these nursery-rhyme rhythms.

'How's it going?' I'd ask, sleepily.

'Going. Going. Gone.'

'How's Toby?'

'Toby jug, we're unplugged, bed bug…'

'Jayne, I have to get up in four hours.'

'Giddy-up, horsey, it's blackberry stirrup.'

'Goodnight, Jayne.'

My sister appeared at the door, tea towel over her shoulder. I was shocked at the shadows under her eyes. She was thinner too.

'Toby, how many times have I told you?' she said. 'You're not to open the door on your own. Go and finish your dinner.'

'I hate peas.'

'Do as I say.'

'But—'

'Go! *Now*.'

A touch over the top, I thought. I gave her a hug. 'Rory home yet?'

Jayne shook her head with a shallow smile and took my bag. I followed her down the corridor, my shoes clunking on the timber.

I was seven, Jayne 12, when our mother was killed in a car accident. Our father had been at the wheel. Not long after, he hired a live-in house-keeper – the sour and hard Doreen – while he quietly disconnected. Doreen's caustic, critical tongue bypassed me and found its soft target in my sister. Jayne was forced to clean the bathrooms, make all the beds (with hospital corners), get me to and from school, and help me with my homework. I looked up to my sister, did everything she told me to.

The spare room overlooked a pond and I listened to the frogs while I unpacked. The single bed was a dark timber and the patchwork quilt be-longed to my childhood. I was hanging my dress up in the lowboy when I heard Jayne's voice raised in the kitchen. I ventured out to see her pushing a spoonful of peas against Toby's closed lips.

'Eat them.'

Toby shook his head.

Jayne reached over and pinched his nose, forcing him to open his mouth for air. Then she shoved the spoon in.

'Keep your mouth closed,' she warned, 'and chew.'

Toby's tongue showed a mass of lumpy green as he began to cry. Jayne grasped his lower jaw and worked it up and down.

'Why are you doing that?' I asked.

'None of your business,' she said, her eyes avoiding mine.

When Rory arrived home, he gave me a peck on the cheek before disappearing with a beer. I'd been living in London working in pubs when Jayne met and married Rory. I had a hunch it was her first relationship. If she'd had boyfriends at school, I was unaware of them. By the time I reached my teenage years, when Jayne was monitoring my 'firsts' (tongue kiss, boob grope, genital touch), she was almost past them.

Then the surprise that was Toby arrived. Jayne and Rory moved south, where it was more affordable, but Rory found it difficult to pick up local work and was forced to commute to Sydney.

In the kitchen, Jayne told me with a sidelong glance that she'd invited their plumber to dinner.

'Tell me you haven't,' I said, with a groan.

'Wouldn't it be great if you hit it off and moved down here too?'

'I'm a city gal, sis.'

'So was I,' she said, with a lip-curl. 'Once.'

The plumber was chatty enough, but there was little to connect us, apart from discussing *The Block*. The odd thing was how Toby took to him, lingering by his chair before heading off to bed. I caught him gazing at the man's muscled arms, his shiny white joggers, and wondered what the attraction was.

Next morning I woke to screaming outside my window. I drew back the curtains. The game in the backyard brought a smile to my face – a nude Toby fleeing from Jayne and the hose. But my smile froze when I realised he was shivering and crying.

'Your sheets were wet again, weren't they?'

'Yes,' Toby sobbed.

'You make me wash them every morning.'

'Sorry, Mummy.'

I grabbed my cardigan and raced out the back door. 'What are you doing?' I knocked the hose from Jayne's hands, wetting us both. 'Are you mad?'

'Mad?' she said, with a laugh. 'Mad? This is known as *parenting*. What would you know about it?'

'Where's Rory?' I asked, as I turned off the tap. I wrapped the trembling Toby in my cardigan.

'Gone to work,' said Jayne, looping the hose into a neat coil. 'He's useless anyway.'

The three of us headed into the house, Toby clinging to me, hiccupping.

'How about a nice warm Milo?' I kissed his wet curls.

'I'll decide what he can and can't have, thank you,' said Jayne.

The day cleared blue and crisp. Jayne hummed over our bowls of porridge as though everything was normal. She treated Toby to fingers of toast with Nutella. Warm and dry in a red fleecy top, Toby munched quietly, swinging his legs. Later, we wandered down to the local markets, stopped for coffee, bought an organic chook and some vegetables for dinner and strolled back singing 'Baa, baa, black sheep' over and over, Toby's hands nestled in ours. He appeared cheerful and lively, like any four-year-old.

Once we were back at the house Jayne closed her bedroom door for a nap, leaving Toby and me to our own devices. He led me to his room where we undertook the construction of a small Lego town. I was full of wonder at his skills. He chattered away, building turreted buildings, motoring small figures up and down his doona, pulling apart coloured bricks with his teeth. His curls gleamed bronze in the sunlight slanting in the window. After a time, we tiptoed out to the kitchen for refreshments, careful not to wake Jayne. I handed him a cup of apple juice, and when it slipped out of his grasp, clattering to the floor, he stiffened, pupils wide.

'Sorry, sorry, sorry.'

'Hey,' I said, 'it's okay, Toby. We can clean it up.'

'Quick,' he said, running to check on Jayne's bedroom door, still closed. 'Quick,' he whispered, trotting back.

'Toby, nothing's broken, and look – the floor's clean now. It's okay.'

In the afternoon I found Jayne in the kitchen stuffing the chicken. A pumpkin and a scattering of potatoes lay on the benchtop.

'Can I peel those for you?' I asked.

'Lovely,' she said. Her face was flushed. She raised her glass of white wine. 'Like one?'

'Sure.'

I picked up the peeler and glanced over at Toby in the corner of the couch engrossed in TV. 'Jayne,' I said, and paused. I wasn't sure how to approach this. I'd grown up with my sister looking out for me, not the other way around. She was the one who was always in control. I decided to leap in. 'Do you think you might be having trouble coping?'

'Everything's fine.'

'But hosing Toby like that. Force-feeding him peas. What's it all about?'

'What would you know? You don't have kids.' She gulped down her wine and poured another. I noticed her hand shaking.

'I know I don't have kids—'

'You live your exciting city life, no responsibilities. Have you ever been responsible for *anything*?' she said, her voice rising. She put down her glass and ran to Toby, lifting him up off the couch and covering his face with kisses. 'Love you, love you, *love* you,' she exclaimed.

Toby held himself stiff, and when released rubbed his palm up and down his cheek. Jayne waltzed back into the kitchen, casting me a look of triumph.

I placed the chopped vegetables in a pan and covered them with water. I tried a different tack. 'You and Rory seem distant,' I ventured. 'Are you two—'

'Everything's fine,' she said firmly, turning to switch on the oven.

I gave up and offered to give Toby his bath. Jayne readily agreed, clearly keen to get rid of me.

I perched on the edge of the tub. I decided to talk to Rory, since I was getting nowhere with Jayne. As Toby undressed, I stealthily scanned his body for any marks. None.

When Rory arrived home he joined us in the lounge room. He stood to one side, holding a beer, feet set apart. Toby sat between Jayne and me on the couch, watching a show on African wildlife.

'What did you do today?' Rory asked Toby.

'Stuff,' said Toby, eyes glued to the stalking tiger.

'What?'

'Stuff,' repeated Toby, louder.

'Oh,' said Rory. 'Stuff.'

'We went to the markets, didn't we?' I said, ruffling Toby's curls.

'Amazing,' said Rory.

'It was fun,' I said.

'And how was Mummy today?' said Rory, glancing at Jayne, who hadn't said a word, hadn't looked at him. 'Practically perfect in every way?'

With no dinner guest that evening, Rory made an attempt to keep the conversation going, asking about my time in London, and about my dog. Jayne barely ate, but continued to top up her wine. For dessert she pulled a burnt apple pie from the oven and tossed it into the sink.

'Four and twenty black...black...black,' she intoned, stabbing the pie with a knife.

Rory banged his glass down and pushed himself away from the table, knocking over his chair.

In the morning I found my sister lying beneath the clothesline lining up pegs, pinks in one row, blues in another. A magpie was eyeing her from above, beak at an angle. I knelt beside her.

'Let me help you with the washing.'

'Why can't I do it?'

'You can,' I said. 'You need help though.'

She pressed her forehead to my arm. 'I hate failure.'

'You're tired,' I said, stroking her hair. 'Overwhelmed. You don't have to do it all your own, you know.'

Jayne closed her eyes for a moment, then flipped them open.

'Was I mean to you growing up? Did you hate me?'

'Of course I didn't hate you,' I said. 'You were my whole world. Anyway, it would have been ten times worse without you. Imagine if it was just Dad and Dor*een*.' I made a face.

'You always did what you were told. Not like Toby.'

'He's four, Jayne!'

She got to her feet. Side by side we pegged out the washing.

After breakfast I walked to the hardware store with Rory, leaving Jayne and Toby at home. I asked Rory if he thought Jayne was finding motherhood difficult.

'No idea,' he said, without looking at me. 'She doesn't talk to me anymore. I've stopped asking.'

'So, you're opting out?'

'Give me a break.' He didn't shout, but it was close. 'My job's no picnic, either,' he said. 'And the bloody commute's a killer.'

'Yes, but Toby.'

'What about him?'

'How do you think he's doing?'

He shrugged. 'Seems alright to me. Normal, if that's what you mean. I don't get to see a lot of him, tell you the truth.'

We continued to the shops in silence. Perhaps I was mistaken. You'd think a father would know his own child. I left him at the store and picked up a coffee for my sister.

When I opened the gate I heard a cry. Then another. I raced up the path to find the front door locked. The back door too. I peered through the kitchen window. Toby was on a stool and Jayne was cutting his hair. It seemed normal enough, until I saw the beads of blood on his ears. I banged on the window. Toby was crying. His legs were wriggling, but he was strapped into an old highchair.

'Jayne!' I called, trying to sound normal. 'Let me in. I have coffee.'

She opened the door. Her mouth was a grim line and there were red patches on her neck.

'What's going on?' I asked. My heart was whacking against my chest.

'I'm giving him a haircut,' she said, holding up the clippers. 'What does it look like?'

I pushed her aside and unstrapped Toby as quickly as I could. Jayne watched without saying a word, without trying to stop me.

'My ears hurt,' said Toby. 'Mummy was too hard wif the clippers.'

'They slipped, Toby,' said Jayne. 'It was an accident, you silly.'

I dabbed at the spots of blood on Toby's ears with a tissue. 'Doesn't look like an accident,' I muttered.

Jayne moved to the sink. She twisted the taps on full bore and squirted great gobs of Palmolive into the water. Foam billowed over the rim. I watched in disbelief as she clashed the plates. It was like she'd completely blanked out what had just happened. I had no choice. I needed to get through to Rory.

Jayne and Toby were feeding the chooks at the bottom of the yard, Toby scooping out the grain from the pail Jayne held for him. It was the picture of harmony. I headed over to the shed, feeling a flicker of self-doubt. I didn't have any expertise in this area. Maybe all mums experienced bad days, and children, most people were fond of saying, were resilient. I shook myself out of it, thinking of everything I'd seen.

Rory was sorting nails and screws into compartments in a storage cabinet. He didn't look up when I came in.

'We need to talk,' I said.

'Oh, geez,' he said. 'Let me guess. Motherhood?'

'Actually,' I said, 'yes, it's about motherhood. There are things I don't think you're aware of.'

'Things?' Rory slid one compartment in and pulled open another. He tore at a pack of screws. His expression hadn't altered – still a frowning concentration on nails and screws.

'So, what do you think?' I said, growing impatient.

'Think?'

He was like little Sir-bloody Echo.

'About Jayne,' I said. 'Maybe you could take her to see someone. Get some help. She's so isolated.'

'Look,' said Rory, slamming the drawer shut. 'I'm the one working my arse off. She wanted to stay at home.'

'But what about Toby?'

'What about him?'

'I think.' I paused. 'I think he's at risk.' My heart was pounding.

He finally looked at me, and for a long time said nothing. His shoulders sagged. He took a deep breath and let it out slowly. 'You don't know what you're talking about,' he said.

I stood staring at him, utterly lost for words. In the pond outside, the frogs had begun their evening chorus. I was working out what to say next when there was a shout from the house. I turned and raced out of the shed.

I found Jayne in the laundry, jumping up and down, pointing at the dryer on the wall. My first thought was that maybe it was on fire, or had come loose. But Rory had done a good job with the screws. It was sturdy, secure. I looked through the little round window. Toby's knees were over his head, his back curved into an excruciating C. A thin little voice was saying, 'Help me, Aunty Karen.'

'What have you done?' I yelled. I opened the dryer door.

'He climbed in when I wasn't looking!'

I reached in and grasped one of Toby's legs. There wasn't enough room to untangle him. He was stuck.

'He looks just like a baby!' My sister's hand covered her mouth, half-suppressing a laugh. 'Just like a baby in the womb!'

Rory appeared in the doorway and stood staring up at the dryer. I shook him by the shoulders.

'Can't you *do* something, you useless fuck?' I pulled my phone from my pocket and dialled emergency. 'We'll get you out, Toby,' I said. 'Don't worry. I'm calling for help. We'll get you out.'

Jayne gazed up at her son. 'This is how it was,' she whispered. 'This is exactly how it was. It was all so simple then. Why did everything have to change?'

The valley was dense with chill. In the brightly lit ambulance Toby held fast to my fingers. They were taking him to hospital for a thorough check-over. Jayne wanted to go, but Toby grew hysterical when she climbed into the ambulance. I put my arm around her and walked her back to the house. I'd help her later, I told her, but for now Toby came first. I told her I'd stay overnight at the hospital, if necessary. I'd stay with Toby as long as I was needed. I wouldn't let him out of my sight. She listened, head bowed, without saying a word, as though I was giving her complicated directions. All this time, Rory had stayed slumped on the couch, saying *fuck* again and again into the hands that covered his face.

They'd dismantled the dryer to get Toby out. Only its shell remained on the wall, gaping.

The Right Moment

You don't go down on me anymore.

Makes me gag, she said. I hate it. Always have.

I do it to you.

You probably like it.

What if I stopped?

I wouldn't whine about it. I'd respect your decision.

Right. That's it, he said. I'm not doing it anymore.

Fine. No biggie.

He sat up, adjusted his pillow and picked fluff off his chest hair. But seriously, he said. It's something we do *for* each other. It's a gift. It's intimate. And loving.

You're really making a case for it, aren't you? She rubbed lotion onto her elbows, sniffed her hands. I love this. Smell it. Jules gave it to me. She said her mum gave it to her and the scent reminds her of things she doesn't want to be reminded of, so she wanted to get rid of it.

Floral.

You didn't even smell it.

I can smell it from here.

In a strop now?

No. He picked up a magazine.

Sorry if I offended your male pride.

Oh, Jesus.

It's…how can I put it? It's like a service.

You appear to enjoy it.

What, because of the moaning? I don't want to pretend anymore. I don't think pretence does our relationship any favours.

He flicked the pages of the magazine. What I don't understand, he said, tossing it aside, is why you never told me before now. I mean, why now?

What's wrong with now? She swung her feet to the floor and padded over to pick up the remote.

You're watching TV *now*?

Women's singles final is on.

They won't even be on the court. Then there's the warm-up.

I like the walk-along-the-corridor part. Then they come out and the crowd cheers and they get a massive bunch of flowers. I choke up watching it.

Well you can skip it this year.

Pardon?

We haven't finished talking.

I can talk and watch at the same time.

Don't turn it on.

Excuse me? What's with the tone?

I'm not one of your pupils, goddammit. He flung back the covers and leapt out of bed. Grabbed the remote from her and hurled it at the wall. The back flew off and the batteries clattered to the floor.

She watched them roll under the TV stand. Bloody hell. All because I won't give you a blow job? She backed away as he moved towards her.

He pulled up short. That's not what this is about, he said.

Well, what *is* it about?

I've been offered a job in Bahrain, he said. I've been trying to find the right moment to tell you. They want my answer tomorrow.

You can't be serious, she said. I'm head teacher next term. No more face to face. Plus, a pay rise. You *knew* that. She picked up the batteries and carefully slotted them back into the remote. Are you trying to tell me – as usual I have to fill in the blanks – are you trying to tell me you intend to go on your own?

Wrong way round, he said.

What?

The negative and positive ends are the wrong way round.

Story of our lives, she said. She rubbed her forehead. I'm tired.

Let's sleep on it.

No. I'm *tired*.

She aimed the remote at the TV then struck it with her palm. What the hell's the matter with this thing? The match will be underway. I've missed the flower-giving. I love the sight of them in their crisp whites, not a bead of sweat. Bags full of racquets. Power in their legs, hope in their hearts. The world's eyes on them. What a moment. I *can't* have missed it.

Home Fires

Megan grabbed a handful of Jatz from the kitchen and went to knock on her mother's door. 'Come on, Mum,' she said. 'Open up. Aren't you hungry?' She tried the handle. 'Mum?'

How long would it be this time?

She could hear Mrs Layton calling for her dog next door. 'Peachie!' The rattle of dry pellets into a metal bowl. 'Peachie!'

The house was cold. Megan went to her room and took off her uniform and pulled on some track pants and a fleecy top.

She found a can of spaghetti in the pantry. Jeremy's, of course. Not much of a contribution when he hung around here all day, every day. Taking long showers. Leaving the heater on. And now he'd gone without a word.

Megan was glad he'd gone – he made her feel uncomfortable in her own home. And her mum was always putting on a display, laughing too loud and swinging her hips around. Everything he said was *so funny*. Megan's skin crawled when Jeremy was here.

Her mum was hibernating the way she always did when they left. She'd emerge after a couple of days, like some sort of abject night creature. Megan would bring her cups of tea and sit brushing her hair and stroking her cheek, saying little.

She tipped the spaghetti into a saucepan. The cat mewed around her ankles.

'Sorry, puss. No milk.'

Before Jeremy was Harry. Harry smelt of turf and bourbon. Megan would come home from school to find them passed out on the couch, her mum's top slipping off her shoulders, Harry's chest with its sparse hairs, his man-boobs. She'd fling open the doors and windows to let out the stench.

'Whaa-the?' they'd mutter from the couch.

Then there was the pale, strange David with his Basset-hound eyes and bony hands. Her mum had taken care of David, who seemed new to the world, and grateful, as if she'd served him the last bowl of soup on the planet.

Megan stirred the bubbling spaghetti, then took the pan to the couch, where she sat eating it with a spoon, staring at her reflection in the darkened window.

She woke when the phone rang. She looked down at the pan on the floor beside her. The cat had licked it clean. She couldn't remember pulling the rug over herself. The answering machine clicked on. *Babe, can you pick up? Babe. I need some money. Can yez do a transfer? Two hundred. I'm stranded.*

Jeremy. The phone rang again and again. Each time the message was nastier. Megan took the phone off the hook.

She went to her mother's room, pressing her ear to the door.

'Mum, I'm going to bed,' she called. 'Can I get you anything?' She heard the bed creak. No light under the door. 'Night, Mum,' she said.

She picked up the cat and buried her nose in its fur. 'You can sleep with me tonight, puss.'

The doorbell chimed as Megan was drawing the curtains. Her heart jumped. What if it was Jeremy coming for money? He'd be pissed off he couldn't get through on the phone. She needed to think of a story. Her mum was sick, really sick, and the ambulance was on its way. That'd scare him off.

She peeped through the chink in the curtain. Phew. It wasn't Jeremy. It was someone with a beard. She called through the closed door: 'Who is it?'

'Hi, I'm Mrs Layton's son. My mum's your neighbour. She's looking for her dog, Peachie. The little terrier. Maybe you've seen it?'

'No,' called Megan. 'Sorry. I haven't seen any dog.'

She peeped through the curtain again. Saw the man scratch his beard and turn to go.

'Okay,' he called. 'Thanks, anyway.'

'Wait a minute, hon.' Her mum was standing at her bedroom door, tying the sash round her blue satin robe. 'Open it,' she said, smoothing back her hair and smiling. 'Invite the man in.'

RSVP

The bus was standing room only. Kate studied the hair in front of her – a perfectly shaped, lustrous black bob. Recently, she'd noticed her own natural colour fading. She was trying to accept it, celebrate it even, but last night she'd caved in, nipping out to the chemist for a packet of Summer Gold. Too risky to go grey into the world today. She was meeting Simon from RSVP. He'd suggested an open-air café at Circular Quay.

Waking this morning to the garbage truck wheezing up the laneway, the insistent sun pressing at the curtains, Kate had been tempted to cancel and hole up in her flat. But the final step in her three-step plan was to make contact, to start dating. And, she reminded herself, it was only a coffee, only a morning.

The girl with the black hair was wearing Doc Martins, fishnet tights and a short purple skirt, reminding Kate of her student days. Today, she'd gone for the business look, but now felt uncertain. Her skirt was a touch too long, too wide. She should have bought classy pumps instead of sandals. At least her blouse was a crisp white, the red beads a jaunty touch. Nothing she could do about it now.

The bus braked at the uni stop. Kate bumped into the black-haired girl, who released her hand on the pole, leaving a damp mark and a waft of sandalwood. Kate apologised.

'No worries,' said the girl, adjusting her daypack and hopping off the bus.

To settle her nerves Kate decided to get off at Wynyard and walk the rest of the way. There was plenty of time. Simon had a window of 45 minutes, his email said, before he had to leave for a conference in Melbourne. A high-pressure job by the sounds of it.

Kate walked past the underground with its smell of stale train-metal and baked goods. People hurried across George Street in suits and smart shoes, carrying briefcases, takeaway coffees. People with purpose. The buildings cast their long, cool shadows as she dawdled.

At the Essex Street crossing, two girls in drill shorts and hiking boots, bearing hefty backpacks, drew up alongside her.

'Excuse me,' one of them said, with an accent. 'How do we get to King's Cross?'

'Pardon?' said Kate, her mind still on people with purpose.

'Apparently Kings Cross has a lot of cheap Backpackers,' the other girl explained.

How healthy they looked, their sun-bleached hair swept up into ponytails, skin clean and clear. Their long thighs were flecked with golden hairs. Kate pointed towards Circular Quay, telling them they could catch a train or a bus.

When the lights changed, the girls crossed with Kate and introduced themselves as Britta and Anna.

'Are you on your way to work?' asked Anna, and Kate's spirits lifted a little. Her outfit must be suitable after all.

'No,' she said. 'I'm meeting someone for coffee.'

Their fresh sweat smelt like bitter summer flowers.

'Girlfriend? Boyfriend?'

Kate was struck by their unabashed openness, their self-confidence. Maybe she should add a fourth step to her pact: travel. Not yet. First things first. 'Neither,' she confessed, and before she could stop herself she'd told them about Simon. In a way it was a relief, when she hadn't even told her mother, who was suspicious of RSVP, saying it was an unnatural way to meet someone. Perhaps it was easy because they were strangers. 'He works in finance,' she said. 'Hardly my strong point.'

'How will you know him?' asked Anna.

Both girls seemed excited by her little adventure; it was hard to resist them.

'He said he'd be holding an iPad with a red cover.'

They arrived at the quay as the Manly ferry was pulling out in a reek of diesel, bundled with ropes and commuters.

'The buses to Kings Cross go from there, the trains from up there,' said Kate. She checked her watch. Eight-thirty. She'd planned a secret walk-by, to see if she could spot Simon from a distance. Decide to go or stay.

'You look nervous,' said Britta.

'Do you want us to wait? He could be a weirdo.'

Oh, why not? thought Kate. She liked these two, with their free-and-easy manners, and could use the encouragement.

The three of them strolled along the harbour foreshore, towards the Museum of Contemporary Art.

'First time you've been on an internet date?' asked Britta, as they sat on a bench in front of the museum.

Kate nodded. First date in 27 years, she thought, internet or otherwise.

This is what she knew about Simon: divorced for a year, a teenage son he saw on weekends. No mention of his ex. Kate hadn't disclosed much, either. There was nothing about her marriage she was inclined to share. And the three years following the divorce were dismal, too dark for comment.

The first two steps in Kate's three-step plan – to stop drinking and begin her TAFE course – had been ticked off. Now it was time to bring some *amour* into her life.

'I'll go and check – red iPad, you say?'

Anna strode off to look for Simon before Kate could stop her. In a few moments she returned. 'He's here,' she said, her face lit with a grin. 'And, Kate, it's your lucky day. I don't think he's a serial killer!'

Oh, thought Kate. She half-wished he hadn't shown up. She'd been mulling over the countless hours spent wandering through art galleries as a student. She took in the boats on the harbour, the tourists on the promenade snapping photos. She felt almost faint. Stay strong, she told herself. Today – with the hair dye, the lipstick, the outfit – it was all about her pact.

'How do I look?'

'Scared,' said Britta. 'Take a deep breath. Relax.'

There he was, tapping his iPad.

'Simon?' Kate palmed down her skirt, billowing in the warm breeze. Her tongue felt thick. Do men stand up for women these days? she wondered.

'Kate,' said Simon, briefly raising his eyes. 'Sit down. I won't be a sec.'

She pulled out a chair, glancing at the girls, who'd wandered over and were casually leaning against the harbour railing.

'Friends of yours?' said Simon, flipping shut the red cover.

'Not exactly,' said Kate. 'I've just met them. They're from Germany.'

'Ask them to join us, if you like.'

Not such a bad idea, thought Kate. Might help calm her down. She waved the girls over. As Simon dragged across extra chairs she took in his appearance. Thick hair, a faded ginger. Lips full and pale. Not exactly good-looking, but sensuous. He wore a dark blue suit.

'We won't stay long,' Britta was saying. 'You two should get acquainted, and anyway we're on our way to Kings Cross.'

'Here's a thought,' said Simon. 'Stay for a coffee, then I'll give you both a lift to the Cross before I head to the airport.'

The girls ordered espressos, Kate a flat white. She noticed the way Simon's gaze kept flitting towards Anna, who was describing a night in a mixed-dorm in Cairns. A British guy had tumbled out of the bunk above and crawled into bed with her. Anna had shoved him onto the floor, where he'd snored the rest of the night in his threadbare undies.

'The weird thing was,' said Anna, 'he'd told us in the pub he was in love with this environmentalist from Surrey. A guy called Brian!'

Kate could see that Simon was fascinated by the story, and by Anna's bra-less, small breasts.

'How about you, Britta?' He exaggerated the 'r' in her name. 'Any romance?'

'No,' said Britta, abruptly. 'I'm getting married in May.'

Kate felt she needed to contribute. Pact: make contact. 'What does your job involve?' she asked. She tried to sound interested.

Simon turned to her. 'Raising billions for different companies, sniffing the occasional backside and getting paid for it. It's a living.'

Kate waited for him to continue. She tidied the sweetener sachets.

'You?' said Simon. 'You mentioned studying?'

'Yes, I'm studying. It's a TAFE course—'

'Waiter,' he said, clicking his fingers. 'Gone to Brazil for the coffee beans?' He looked at Kate. 'You were saying?'

'It's a TAFE course,' Kate repeated, 'on information technology.'

'About bloody time,' said Simon, when the coffees arrived. He turned to Anna. 'Got any more of those juicy backpacker stories?'

A drop of coffee splashed onto Kate's white blouse. An ugly spot. She dabbed it with a paper napkin, arranged her red beads to conceal it. Conscious of warm fingers on her arm, she glanced up to see sympathy in Britta's eyes. Kate gave a weak smile and a small shrug. This was so wrong, she thought. She looked around again at the busy quay. A young woman in a smart suit and sheer stockings hurried past their table with a takeaway cup. A couple in white joggers and polyester jackets called 'We're here!' to a man aiming a camera at them. A high-school boy in a blazer greeted another with a hug. These were people following threads, thought Kate. A thread to an office, a coffee shop, a bus, a ferry, an embrace. She had no thread to follow. Somewhere near the ferry terminal she heard the rumble of a didgeridoo. Why was she sitting here with this strange and arrogant man, spilling coffee on herself? The banners above the museum flapped lazily. She wanted to step over its polished floors in her new summer sandals. She wanted to savour the artworks and sculptures in all their colours and contours. A different type of contact, but kinder.

She stood up. For the first time Simon looked at her directly.

'What's up?'

Kate turned to the girls and shook their hands. 'Lovely to meet you. I hope you enjoy Sydney. Best of luck.'

'Was it something I said?' asked Simon.

Kate slung her bag over her shoulder and pushed in her chair. 'Have a pleasant flight,' she said to Simon. '*Not* terribly nice meeting you.'

She smiled as she walked away. That took the wind out of his arrogant sails, she thought. Hope his mouth catches flies.

Kate sat on the bench in front of the museum, inhaling the briny scent of the harbour. She watched as Simon stood to help Anna on with her backpack. Off to the Cross, by the looks of it. Oh, well. Good luck to them all. The didgeridoo played in the distance. She was content to sit there enjoying the scenery until the museum opened. A seagull landed at her feet and she told it she had no chips.

Moored alongside the promenade was a small cruise boat. Kate idly watched the passengers climbing aboard. Divine day for a cruise, she thought – the tourists were in luck. The harbour was a glassy green, the bridge and the Opera House postcard perfect. Onto the gangway stepped two figures bearing backpacks. Long, tanned legs. Bleached hair in ponytails. Kate shook her head, puzzled. Britta and Anna?

The two travellers made their way to the bow, unloaded their packs, and turned towards Kate. Even from afar, Kate could tell they were grinning. The girls began waving at her with big, sweeping arcs, calling *Hello! Kate! Hello!* Kate hesitated for the briefest moment, then raised her hand high above her head and waved back, laughing.

Lost

Mrs Lewis opened the door, brushing a crumb from her mouth.

'Sorry to bother you,' said Amanda, 'but has my little boy been here? Oscar? You know the one. About this tall. Straight, light-brown hair. Skinny legs.' She tried to keep the panic out of her voice. Jesse hugged her leg below her skirt. He wasn't well; she could feel his fevered forehead against her skin.

'He came in for a while,' said Mrs Lewis. 'Ray had a chat to him, didn't you, Ray?' she called down the corridor.

'What's that?'

'The boy who was here. You chatted to him.'

'Yep.'

'Could I speak to Mr Lewis, please? May I come in?'

Amanda slung Jesse onto her hip and followed the woman down the pink corridor and into the kitchen. She had to be vigilant with Oscar, even though he was almost seven. He'd hurtle down the hill, whooping and joyous, and she'd have to call out for him to brake at the kerb. But he hadn't run off since he was a toddler.

Mr Lewis sat at the table in his singlet, the newspaper in front of him folded into a narrow rectangle. The small black and brown terrier under his chair raised its head, growling softly.

'Quiet, girl,' he said. 'Molly's old and cranky. She doesn't like strangers.' He didn't look at Amanda as he spoke, instead keeping his eyes on the form guide. 'But she didn't mind the boy. He said it'd be fun to have a dog. Said his dad didn't want one.'

'How long was he here?'

'How long would you say, Meg? Twenty minutes?'

'Twenty. Maybe 15.'

The radio on the table was tuned to the races. The café curtains shifted in the breeze from the table fan.

'Then what?' Amanda heard the impatience in her own voice.

'Eh?'

'Then what did he do? Where did he go?'

'He didn't go home?'

'No.'

'Dunno then. Said he was going home.'

Amanda waited for more. Through the screen door she could see the clouds making their slow passage and the vast branches of a jacaranda specked with mauve, set to bloom.

'Well, thanks. I'll keep looking.'

'Tried the park?' said Mr Lewis, still not looking up.

'Pardon?'

'Tried the park? I told him I used to play down there as a boy. Remember finding a bluetongue under a rock.'

'Thanks,' Amanda said, her heart lifting.

'He seems to like animals,' he added. 'Should get him a dog.'

Amanda studied the arrangement of sticks dug deep into the soft soil under the old gum, so typical of one of Oscar's games. It could be a fort, or a battlefield. As she touched each stick in turn, she thought she felt the remnant heat from his hands.

'Oscar here?' Jesse asked.

'No, Oscar's not here, but I think he's been playing here.' She stood up.

A child's red drink bottle lay under the picnic table. Amanda picked it up, brushed off the dirt and put it on the table. 'Come on, let's hurry. Daddy will be home by now.'

'What the fuck do you mean he's gone missing?' Todd pulled the fridge door open and took out a beer. He tossed the bottle top into the sink where it clattered on the stainless steel. At the small, fierce sound Amanda's stomach twisted.

'I fell asleep when Jesse was having a nap. Oscar went next door, to the Lewises'. Then he went to the park.'

'How do you know?'

'Sticks – stuck in the ground in a pattern. It could only be Oscar. Let's call the police.'

'No. Waste of time. We'll look for him ourselves.'

Even with this we haven't touched each other, thought Amanda. She'd watched TV programs about missing children. The parents would often split at some stage during the interminable search and wait. *The search for Tommy took its toll on the marriage and Bill and Marian went their separate ways in 2006.* She imagined Bill and Marian dealing separately and in private with their grief, imagined them fighting with each other, the pain exploding. The silences. It would be like that with her and Todd. The deep lines on the back of his neck creased as he lifted the beer to his mouth. Weathered and flushed, his skin seemed thicker.

Jesse had been grizzling since coming home from the park.

'What's the matter with him?'

She picked him up, kissing his forehead. 'He's not well.'

'Give him some Panadol. Let's go.'

As they drove around the neighbourhood, Amanda tried to keep her mind off horror scenarios: Oscar bleeding, Oscar with a leg broken, Oscar beaten up, Oscar abducted. She was sick with fear, but none of this she shared with her husband.

'We should have rung the police.'

'I told you. Waste of time. Cops are hopeless. Why the fuck did you go to sleep?'

'I was exhausted,' said Amanda. 'Up on the hour all night with Jesse. He's sick, remember?'

She knew Todd would only have been dimly aware of her getting up. Things were different now. In the early days, when the newborn Oscar slept in their bedroom Todd had often suggested she get a night's rest in the spare room. He'd bring the baby in to her to feed. Afterwards he'd change him and settle him back into the crib. Amanda used to just roll into her pillow and go back to sleep. Since Jesse's arrival, everything had changed. Jesse had screamed from birth. Feeding was a nightmare. He'd pull off her breast as though the milk burned him. Her days blurred as she tried to cope with a fractious baby and a wild four-year-old. Todd began to open a beer as soon as he came home from work and then retreat to his office. Somewhere along the way they'd dropped hands and begun to press on solo.

They were driving along the coast road now. The last of the sun glowed on the headland. Todd gripped the top of the wheel, his head jutting forwards as he scanned the bike path. A girl on a bike with training wheels was riding straight-backed ahead of her father, her handlebars a rainbow of streamers.

'I think we should go down to the beach,' said Amanda, as they passed their usual track. 'He might be down there. If he's crying, we can't hear him from the car.'

Todd pulled over. 'Go on then.'

'What?'

'Get out. I'll keep driving with Jesse.'

'Mummy!' said Jesse. 'Me come wif you.'

But when Amanda got out Todd pulled the door shut and drove away with Jesse. She watched the car disappear round the bend. Then she picked her way down the cliff path to the beach, thinking how Oscar loved to race down it with his glorious battle cry. She removed her sandals and looked up and down the darkening sand. A dog silhouetted against the sea bounded after a ball, its owner following with a curved thrower. A lone jogger traced the firm shoreline, dodging the incoming tide. Amanda headed for the shrubbery on the dunes, Oscar's favourite hideout. She called his name again and again.

When the sand squeaked behind her she turned hopefully. But it was Todd. She was only just able to make out his face in the gloom.

'Jesse's spewed in the car, we have to go home.'

'And call the police?'

'Would you *shut up* about the police!' Todd grabbed her by the shoulders. His face was an inch from hers. '*Shut up!*' he yelled, letting go of her roughly. Amanda stumbled, hitting her arm against the timber barrier rail.

'I can't stand it.' Todd waved his arms. 'I'm going fucken crazy.'

'Me too!' Amanda yelled back at him. 'Everything's gone to *shit*. All I want is to find him.' She rubbed her arm.

From the car Jesse's cries drifted down the track.

'Come on,' said Todd, in a quieter tone. 'Let's go home. He might be back by now.'

Within minutes Jesse had fallen asleep. They followed the coast road back to town. The streetlights flickered on. As they passed the shopping centre, Amanda recalled shopping with Oscar as a toddler. He'd hide from her, pressing through the folds of dresses on a rack to find a wall no one ever saw, his small hot hands splayed against its cool. She'd be searching the mall, questioning shopkeepers, when he'd dart out from nowhere and tap her on the bottom with a cheeky giggle. She felt her throat tighten and turned her face to the window, rubbing her sore arm again.

'Sorry,' said Todd. 'I want to find him, too. I'm his *father*, for godsake.'

The first thing Amanda saw as she entered the kitchen with a sleeping Jesse in her arms was the answering machine blinking red. She pressed the button.

Hi, Amanda. It's Jane. I just wanted to check that you knew Oscar was here. He said you did. He was pretty hungry, so he's having some dinner. Give me a call when you get in.

Amanda felt herself slide into a place somewhere between relief and hysteria. Todd, who had been standing in the doorway listening to the message, slowly looped the keys over the kitchen hook and turned to go into the living room. He stopped. Amanda saw his shoulders rise and his fingers link across the back of his neck. She didn't go to him, as he hadn't to her. Jesse's head was heavy, his nose buried in her neck. There was the faint acidic smell of vomit.

'I'll call Jane and go and pick him up,' she said at last.

'No,' said Todd. 'I'll pick him up.' He turned and walked back into the kitchen, his eyes big and dark. After a long moment he said, quietly, 'This is no good.'

'No.'

'Why would he go to Jack's without telling you?'

The answer came easily. It was Oscar's refrain: 'Because Jack's house is more fun.'

Todd nodded. He spread his hands flat on the kitchen bench. He leant over them and bowed his head. Amanda saw how rough the skin on his hands was. She saw how grime had settled into the creases of his fingers. No amount of scrubbing could remove it. The only time she'd seen his hands free of it, and softer, was on their honeymoon, when they'd swum and snorkelled daily. It was because of his work, in all weathers; it was the tools, the dust.

She lifted a finger and ran its tip down the vein on the back of his hand. She released it and watched the blood rushing back. Then she reached up, unhooked the car keys and held them out for him.

The Gardener

The new gardener removed his shirt in the February heat, and when he turned to pick up his shovel you could see a snake tattoo twisting all the way down his muscular back to the top of his jeans. Excitement flared in the classroom like magnesium.

'Quiet,' said Ms Grainger. 'Come away from the window, Claire.'

Ms Grainger, fresh from teacher training, was sturdy but timid, with soft skin and pale, frightened eyes. She wore hiking sandals and peasant skirts. Her blouse had damp patches under the arms and when she approached Julia and Claire's workbench there was a smell of wet onions.

'Ms Grainger,' said Claire. 'I forgot to hand in my excursion fees at the office. They're due this morning.'

The teacher flushed. 'As quick as you can.'

Claire winked at Julia. 'Here I come, my muscle-man,' she whispered, tilting her head in the direction of the gardener.

This was new, Claire's interest in men. Julia had been watching her in the mornings chatting to men as they waited at the bus stop in their business suits. The men seemed wary. Afraid their wives or girlfriends might drive past, thought Julia, as she shrank embarrassed to the rear of the shelter.

It was on a bright winter morning in kindy when Claire and Julia had become friends. Claire was furiously chasing a boy across the playground because he'd pinched her arm. Her flying, red-ribboned ponytail – the whole bold, free look of her – immediately captivated Julia. She joined in the chase and together they cornered the boy behind the washrooms. They tickled him, untucked his shirt and tossed his cap onto the roof. The two girls were made to stay in the classroom over lunch and had been friends ever since.

Ms Grainger had seen the gardener remove his shirt too. On the first day of term, when he'd bid her good morning as she made her way towards the staff room, his voice trickled through her like warm honey. She longed to hear it again. He was appearing in her dreams – so fleeting he was gone when she woke, nerves thrumming. She watched now as Claire skipped past him, laughing and flicking her shiny hair in the sunlight. Claire was the sort of girl Ms Grainger had always wanted to be. Adventurous, careless, confident.

The bell rang. Music was next. Julia gathered up Claire's books. They were due to be assessed on their Türk Rondo duet. She raced across the playground to check out-of-bounds. She stuck her head under the bathroom doors. At the discordant sound of tuning instruments, she muttered, 'Shit,' and bounded up the stairs to the music rooms. Claire, already seated at the piano, turned and made saucer eyes at her, as if to say, 'Wait till I *tell* you!'

Throughout the performance, Julia was aware of Claire's state of thrill – she was busting with some kind of news. With only a couple of mistimed notes it was soon over, and at the end of class Claire grabbed Julia's sleeve.

'This tops the lot,' she said. 'This is *major*.'

'What is?' Julia demanded. 'Where were you? I was looking everywhere.'

'Picture this,' said Claire, pausing while her hands framed the forthcoming drama. 'The gardener. And. Rosa Bertoli.'

Julia shook her head, at a loss.

'*Hugging.*' Claire held her breath, watching.

'Where?'

'Behind the tool shed.'

'Are you *sure*?'

'Sure as I'm standing here.'

'Kissing?'

'Dead set.'

Rosa Bertoli had an air of mystery, with Mona Lisa eyes that seemed to look beyond you, thick dark hair, a Cupid's bow mouth and dimples. Her Italian grandfather was a scientist and Rosa too was deeply brilliant, especially in languages and maths. Julia had the feeling Rosa knew more about the ways of the world than any of them. The fact that she had friends at uni only added to her intrigue. Claire, in particular, was always trying to uncover details, but Rosa kept herself to herself.

Claire became obsessed with exposing the liaison. She persuaded Julia to buy condoms from Woolies and slip one between the pages of Rosa's school diary. It fell to the floor when Rosa opened it during science. She snatched it up, but not quickly enough. A slow blush crept up Ms Grainger's neck, like algal bloom. Julia wondered why the teacher didn't say anything or confiscate the condom. She could tell it annoyed Claire, who hissed behind Rosa's back, 'Do you know how to use one of those?'

The girls must suspect, thought Ms Grainger, if they were leaving condoms lying around for her to see. She should take care to conceal her feelings. Nevertheless, she felt drawn to the gardener at lunchtime. He was pruning a bottlebrush, its flush of crimson flowers now sorry and brittle. She sat on a bench close by, and surreptitiously watched him reach through the rough branches, his arms shiny with sweat. If only she were more knowing, bolder, like the girls she taught. The reckless Claire. And

Rosa – so mature, so exotic. Rosa would have no trouble speaking to the gardener. He would pay attention to Rosa.

Julia and Claire strolled past Ms Grainger and sat a short distance away. Claire nudged Julia and held her nose. Julia glanced at Ms Grainger's square sandalled feet on the hot asphalt. She noticed the dark stain from an overripe banana in her brown paper-bag lunch. She saw the teacher sneak looks at the gardener. She saw the gardener speak to her, gesturing up at the sun. Ms Grainger nodded, but appeared to say nothing. It was clear to Julia how the teacher felt.

Claire continued to pursue Rosa. She brought in a brochure on sexually transmitted infections, stuck a note to it – *You never know where his* **** *has been* – and taped it to Rosa's chair. But by the time Rosa came to class it had gone. Ms Grainger held it crumpled in her fist. Her knuckles, Julia noticed, were mauve and pinch-white.

The next step, Claire announced, was to tail her. They followed Rosa home, watched her open the gate with its fancy letterbox, wander into the tidy garden with the Cupid fountain. From the bus shelter across the road they watched her mother bring an espresso to an old man seated in the shade of an ancient maple, a red rug over his knees. Holding a *Cleo* in front of their faces, they watched Rosa kiss both his cheeks and sit beside him. Claire even missed her beloved netball in order to watch Rosa.

'They have to be meeting *somewhere*,' she said.

Julia began to wonder if Claire had imagined the encounter with the gardener. Her doubts grew as they failed to turn up evidence. But Claire was unstoppable, and Julia, as always, rode in her slipstream.

Claire said she was convinced Rosa was pregnant. 'She looks fat, don't you think?'

'Not really. She looks the same to me.'

'Look at her side-on. Look.'

They were leaning against the wall under the school footbridge. Rosa was heading for the circle of shade beneath the jacaranda. She sat on the grass, stretched out her legs and opened a book.

'I wonder why she was away yesterday,' said Claire. 'Morning sickness?'

'I heard her grandfather was rushed to hospital. It might have something to do with that.'

'Stop sticking up for her.'

'I'm not, I just think—'

'What?'

'Nothing.' Julia quailed under her friend's glare.

Claire's methods grew bolder. She drew a cartoon on the whiteboard: a naked man, biceps bulging, gripping a garden spade in front of his privates. Beside him stood a naked woman in sandals with a black thatch of pubic hair, love hearts spilling from her eyes. Claire had just scuttled back to her seat when Ms Grainger arrived for the double period. There was an air of suspense as the girls waited to see how she'd react. She didn't notice it at first. But when she faced the board to mark up the morning's task, her shoulders appeared to slump. She turned to the class, her face drained of colour.

'Who did this?' Her voice was tremulous. Julia thought she might be about to cry.

The class was quiet, apart from the scrape of a chair, the rustle of paper.

'Is someone going to own up?'

Julia found herself hoping that Claire would put her hand up, or that she herself would have the nerve. Instead, Ms Grainger wordlessly erased the cartoon, removed the cap of her whiteboard marker and in uneven script set out the task numbers, one to five.

Claire gave the thumbs up to Julia, who'd been watching Rosa. Rosa's expression had assumed the marble tones of a Florentine statue. Knowing, unknowable. Julia felt she was looking down at them from an ancient perch.

The girls' assignments lay untouched on Ms Grainger's desk at home. She was finding it difficult to concentrate. Her fears about her ability to teach were growing. At school she was constantly on the lookout for nasty notes and drawings. She was constantly hoping the gardener would speak to her, or she would have the courage to speak to him, and this frayed her nerves further.

Claire said she needed to get a reaction from 'Ice Queen Rosa'.

At the swimming carnival all the students were encouraged to participate, whether competent swimmers or not. Claire was talented, twice making it to State in freestyle. Rosa only ever entered the breaststroke; she would never put her face in the water, just a chin-up, white-capped, slightly disdainful lap.

Claire told Julia to buy two white caps, just like Rosa's. They were to jump in, not dive, and then ever so slowly breaststroke up the pool with their heads out, noses in the air, superior expressions on their faces.

The crowd cheered and hooted. The timekeepers didn't bat an eye. As she climbed out of the pool, Julia scanned the stands to see how Rosa had reacted and was glad when there was no sign of her. She hoped she was in the change rooms and had missed the cruel display.

At roll call before boarding the buses, Rosa was missing. Claire was smug. Rosa was in for it now. She'd left without telling the teachers. All the way back to school Claire re-enacted their swim, doubling over with laughter and urging Julia to join in. Julia didn't. An idea had taken hold – that Claire might have invented the whole thing. But she couldn't bring herself to suggest it. She'd never challenge Claire.

The next day Rosa was absent. As was the gardener.

'Oh, my God,' exclaimed Claire in Science. 'This is amazing. This is exactly what we've been waiting for. She'll be sprung, for sure.'

'You don't know,' said Julia, feeling her pulse quicken. 'There's no evidence.'

'Seriously? Take it from me, it's so *obvious*,' Claire said, with a sneer. 'Fuck, I bet they're having a love child. What the hell does he see in her? If only I'd got to him first.' She punched her palm.

'Quiet,' said Ms Grainger from behind their bench. 'Keep your minds on task.'

Julia looked up. Ms Grainger was puffy around the eyes. Julia apologised and asked if she felt unwell. Claire glared at her. Ignoring her, Julia asked again, 'Are you feeling okay, Ms G?'

To everyone's astonishment, Ms Grainger let out a sob and ran from the classroom.

'What the frig was that about?' snarled Claire.

'I thought she looked sick.'

'She always looks bloody sick.'

'Doesn't hurt to be nice sometimes.' Julia picked up her books and walked out.

The next day Rosa was back at school. She'd been at her grandfather's funeral. There was a picture of him in the local paper, a rug draped over his knees.

Ms Grainger was away. They were told the replacement teacher would take the class until the end of term. At recess Julia asked at the office what was wrong, but they wouldn't tell her.

'Why do you want to know?' asked Claire.

Julia looked at Claire, whose face was twisted with annoyance. Instinctively, she knew Claire had been responsible for something, something like a wounding. And she had participated.

The bell rang.

'Art,' said Claire. 'Bludge.' She picked up her bag and took a step.

Julia stayed where she was.

'Come on, what's the matter with you?'

'Tell me the truth,' said Julia. 'Did you really see Rosa with the gardener?'

Claire's eyes narrowed until she was looking through her lashes. Julia waited. Soon a slow smile appeared.

'I've got the *best* plan,' said Claire. 'Come on, I'll tell you about it on the way.'

Julia didn't move. 'You haven't answered me.'

'We're best friends,' said Claire. 'Why would I lie to you?'

Fire Under the Skin

Carl had visited an array of specialists but none could give him an answer. It was like fire ants tunnelling under his skin, he told them. His skin was hot and crawling at the same time.

He'd take long cold showers, emerge mauve and dripping and leave a trail of wet footprints on the carpet. Towelling dry would only set him on fire, he explained to Clara.

It occurred to Clara that the condition was psychosomatic, but instead of suggesting this she continued to buy various items with cooling properties – today it was a bag of crushed ice and a watermelon.

I'll slice it in a sec, she called from the music room. Just give me five. Then you might try an ice-bath.

She ran her fingers up and down the scales. Three days until the concert and she'd not yet mastered the trills. Carl's condition was sapping her energy. Her fingers felt stiff with stress.

Meanwhile, in the next apartment, the bearded man had taken to tap-tap-tapping a strange rhythm in the evenings. Indescribable the effect this was having on the already charged air.

On the day of the concert Clara ran a bath, with the plan to luxuriate in the hot water, flex and unflex her fingers while playing the entire concerto in her head. While the water was running she repaired a button on her dress. Carl was out roaming the neighbourhood, collecting pieces of aloe vera.

What with the intermittent tapping, Carl's skin and her calendar crowded with bookings, Clara felt like an insect in a jar. She loved Carl and perhaps therein lay the problem. *Was* it love? Was this love in fact an inhibitor?

She snipped the black thread and stowed away her sewing basket.

While she was in the bath her manager left a message saying they'd almost filled the seats. For a newcomer this was very promising, he squeaked. He added that the trio from South America booked to appear before Clara had been spotted downing tequilas in the neighbouring bar. Just a heads-up, he said. If they're hammered you'll be the entire show.

Clara listened to the message then lowered her head into the water. What had she been thinking about earlier? About love being an inhibitor. If she put the same amount of energy into her practice and her composing as she did into loving Carl, her career could quite possibly fly.

She ignored the muffled knock at the door at first, but it grew insistent. It might be a delivery – natural or unnatural remedies ordered online. Carl wouldn't appreciate having to collect the package from the depot.

Bathrobe on and hair coiled in a towel, Clara opened the door to see the bearded man from next door. He smiled without showing his teeth. His arms hung straight by his sides.

My name is Jovan. I am neighbour.

I know, said Clara, holding the neck of her robe. Your car space, she said. I've seen you.

Your music. Jovan opened his big hands to the ceiling and moved them side to side. It is very special. To me.

Oh, I'm sorry, said Clara. My music room should be soundproof – *no noise.*

I hear very small. Small sounds.

Where are you from?

Serbia.

Clara nodded. Well. Thank you. You must come to one of my concerts.

That would be special.

If you'll excuse me.

Wait one minute. Jovan reached behind him and placed before her a three-legged wooden stool, topped with a plush red velvet seat rimmed with heavy brass studs. For the music, he said, and with a nudge of his hand he gave the seat a twirl.

At that moment Carl appeared in the corridor with a basket of fleshy cuttings.

Carl, this is our neighbour, Jovan. Look at this divine piano stool he made for me.

Carl grunted and scratched himself. So you're the one making the racket.

Racket?

Noise. Bim, bim.

Yes. Very sorry. Jovan shifted his feet. Well, goodbye. Nice in meeting. Music beautiful, he added.

You were particularly unpleasant to Jovan, said Clara, fastening her earrings.

Carl, stripped down to his shorts, had split open the aloe leaves on the kitchen bench, revealing their jelly innards.

Do my back?

You can't be serious, said Clara. She raised her arms, drawing attention to her black velvet dress.

Carl looked her up and down. Put on an apron. I'm on fire here.

Clara slapped a leaf to his back and smeared it across his skin. You need to get dressed, she said. I'm going to be late.

I can't put a shirt on over this stuff, said Carl. I need to wait until it dries.

Clara tossed the mangled leaf into the sink and wiped her hands.

What about the other leaves? asked Carl. Come on, I'm burning up.

Clara took her purse from the piano. She slowly rotated Jovan's stool, humming the concerto's opening bars. Then she draped her shawl, dusk-red, around her shoulders and opened the door.

Hey! said Carl. Come back. I'm burning here. Burning alive.

Cooking for One

I'm at the counter in the chemist paying for fish oil tablets when I run into him – this long lean man named John with love-in-a-mist-blue eyes from my intro-to-meditation class. In his hand is a packet of Imodium. I'm not sure how to greet someone purchasing an anti-diarrhoea product. My cheeks are burning. I can tell he can't quite place me.

'Om,' I say, middle digit to thumb.

'Of course,' he says. 'Namaste.' He looks down at me, eyes crinkling at the corners.

I'm lost for words. Cancer Council sunglasses scrutinise me from their stand. Furled umbrellas are poised to flower in another.

'Well,' says John, with a sudden and dazzling smile. 'See you Friday.' He takes his little package and his apple green shirt past the croaking frog in the doorway and into the sunlight.

I turn to the assistant and ask for a bottle of St John's Wort for good measure. I'm behaving like a teenager. Are the stars out of whack? Is it menopause? Or perhaps it's just that I haven't been in a man's arms for a long time.

Outside, I stare for some seconds at the empty space that had been John's car. Across the road in the doorway of Camilla's Hairdressing a thin girl in black, her blond hair tipped with chocolate-brown, peers at me over her coffee and I'm aware right then that I just don't fit. I'm 52, but I only know this when I catch sight of myself in shop windows. I stroll around thinking I look the way I did when I was 22, and I'm surprised when a man I have a crush on doesn't stop dead in his tracks when he sees me in the chemist.

I check my watch – 4:30. I'll be late for cooking class. I race for the bus and collapse into a seat. Must pull myself together. Breathe in the good, breathe out the bad. White light in, grey smoke out. I'm getting good at these recoups.

When I arrive, Moira hands me my apron, whispering, 'You haven't missed much.'

I whisper back, 'I just saw your father in the chemist.'

During our round of introductions on day one, Moira had outlined her reasons for taking cooking classes. First – after ignoring her father for three years post-divorce, she was now living with him and wanted to make up for her behaviour by cooking tasty meals. The second reason was that she was planning ahead. She didn't want her kids to get ADHD, which was apparently caused by preservatives and colourings. Forward planning! Only 18. Not even a boyfriend, as far as I knew.

When it was my turn for the reveal I found myself sifting through my reasons. Because my ex-husband was a better cook than I was? Because after three months of going to bed at seven o'clock I'd decided it was time to get out of the house in the evening? In the end I made up a story about neighbourhood get-togethers. I said everyone was taking turns at open-house Sundays, so I needed to learn to cook a half-decent meal.

Truth is, I've reached a point where I wouldn't mind having the neighbours over. Sometimes the evenings are so quiet I swear I can hear the earth settling and breathing. I stare out the lounge-room window into the gathering dusk, at the birds having last-minute parties in the treetops. I listen to the *din-ner!* calls to children. I need to fill my house with noise.

I ask Moira how her Asian Noodle Hotpot turned out.

'Dad loved it. He ate three bowlfuls.'

I smile. That might account for the Imodium. 'What's on the menu today?'

'Orange Beef Stir-fry,' she says, working her whisk. 'We're up to the sauce.'

I set about chopping spring onions. We get to eat our cooking class meals, which means I eat well on Tuesdays. The rest of the week it's pasta, or a boiled egg, or cheese on toast. Jake, my 20-year-old, visits once a week, so I make an effort then. Annie is in London working in a pub. Annie is 22, which is probably why I get on so well with Moira (that and because she's John's daughter, with John's eyes, John's smile).

As I dice a capsicum it occurs to me I should try growing these luscious red bells. Another item on my long list of new ventures since the divorce is a vegie garden. It's astounding how you can wake up in the morning to see a heavy cucumber dangling off the vine where none existed the night before. Too many for one person – this has become apparent. Pickling could well be next on the list.

We line our finished dishes along the bench. Moira's is *perfecto* – the beef has a shiny, rich-brown appearance. My beef looks like scraps of old mushroom. Must have missed a step. Later, we take our meals into the little brick courtyard and gather around an upturned wine barrel and a fat citronella candle to eat and chat about food.

Moira and I catch the bus back together.

By way of conversation, I ask, 'What are you up to tonight?'

'Probably just watch a bit of telly with Dad. Check online for job ads.'

'This morning I saw a notice in Little Italy's window looking for a kitchen hand,' I say. 'How about that?'

Moira studies her nails. 'I have no experience.'

Her self-doubt reminds me of Annie. I pat her arm.

'Listen. You're doing a cooking course. You know how to chop onions, wash dishes, yes?'

'Yes,' she says. 'That's true.' She turns to me and smiles a John's-daughter dazzler.

We study the notice in Little Italy's window.

'Do I look okay?'

Moira always looks neat. Today she's in slim black jeans, sandals and an ice-blue top. Her dark hair is scooped up in a glossy ponytail.

'You look wonderful,' I say, resisting the urge to tell her to stand up straight.

I wait for her on the pavement. I could go for a job like this. An evening job could be the answer. Better than selling scratchies and newspapers all day. *I* can scrub pots and pans. *I* can stack a dishwasher. Watch me call out in my best Italian accent *fettuccine carbonara, pronto!* I picture myself yelling 'Yes, chef!' in the steamy kitchen, collapsing at the end of the shift, booted feet on a chair, holding a glass of house vino, cracking jokes with the waiters. I'd wend my way home to a sleep of exhaustion, feeling like I'd actually contributed in a small way to the workings of the world.

'I start Friday evening,' says Moira, joining me on the footpath. She's holding an official-looking form. Her eyes are lit up.

'Congratulations,' I say. 'That's great.' I put my arm around her shoulders and squeeze. Scratchies will have to do me for now.

'I'll just be stacking the dishwasher at first, but it's something.'

Moira and I go our separate ways. I watch her turn down her little street with its set of tidy townhouses. Then I head up the hill to my place, a wide arc between me and the fence with the crazy dogs. I check the vegie garden on the way to the back door. The bok choy is pocked with holes. In the gloom I peer into the pale stems until I find tiny soft caterpillars that ooze green slime between my thumbnails. I'll have to read up on how to control these.

No messages. I run the shower. I feel grimy after the cooking class and the bus and the walking. I wonder what to have for dinner, and then I remember my revolting Orange Beef Stir-fry.

After the shower, I stand wet-haired in the lounge room and look out over the neighbourhood. It starts to rain so I close the windows. The evening has been successfully filled and I can now place a lid on the thought-jar of shoulds and might-have-beens. I give myself permission to turn in, to creep under the blankets and surrender my thoughts to the night, the cucumbers swelling on the vine, the dew on the grass, the stars. The settling earth.

Night Shift

There's a ring on the breakfast table. It's not mine. It's six o'clock in the morning, and I'm just in from work. My ankles are swollen, I smell rank, and I've drunk too much coffee. I inspect the ring – it's one of those Irish numbers with clasped hands. Gold. I sniff the air. The usual stale, closed-up smell. I fling open the kitchen window, and head down the corridor to the bedroom. Halfway along I hear the rumble of a snore. Well, at least he's home. If he wasn't it wouldn't be the first time. Coral asks me why I stand for it. What can I say? I love Steve. It's as simple as that. Even if I decided to leave, I wouldn't make it as far as the front gate.

He's asleep, sure enough. His arm lies across my side of the bed, like it's ready to enfold me. It looks soft and vulnerable, the underarm hair wispy, dry. I slip out of my uniform and slide alongside him, right into that arm. He pulls me towards him.

'Hi, babe,' he says, drowsily.

I bring my leg up so it's across him, feeling his firm thigh on my crotch. His cock stiffens against my knee.

'Tired?' he mumbles.

'Uh-huh. But not for this.' I climb over him, ready. Now he's awake, I say, 'Whose ring?'

'Sh,' he says, eyes still closed.

'Whose fucking ring?'

'Dunno what you're talking about.'

'On the table. In the kitchen.'

'No idea.' He opens his eyes. 'You really know how to spoil a moment.'

'Likewise,' I say, rolling off.

Coral says that one day there'll be a piece of evidence so obvious, so incontestable, he'll have nowhere to hide. It's precisely then that I'm supposed to corner him. But right now, I need a shower. It's like my skin is spiked I'm so tired.

He's in his work gear pouring me a cup of tea. He's good like that. I glance at the table. The ring's disappeared.

I take a deep breath. 'We have to talk.'

'Gotta go to work, babe.'

'I just want you to know I've had enough. I'm not going to put up with it anymore.' My voice lacks conviction. He edges in close, curls his arm around my waist, and my insides start doing the melt.

'I love it when you do the school teacher with me.'

I twist out of his grasp. 'This time it's not going to work.'

'Isn't it?' he says, moving in to nibble my neck.

I hate my body for betraying me. The flip-flopping in my belly. Why is it that some guys tug at your sexual strings, reeling you in without a struggle, while others – the nicest of all – leave you cold as a bathroom tile?

After he's gone, I sleep for four hours and wake crumpled and cranky. I look in the mirror. A haircut might help. I only have a couple of hours before my power walk with Coral. I dash to Just Cuts in the mall.

'Have you washed your hair in the last 24 hours?' asks Yvonne.

What if I say no? Would she send me home to wash it?

'No.'

'It's an extra 12 dollars.'

I could buy a bottle of good-quality shampoo for that, but I don't have the energy to argue. 'Actually, I just remembered, I did wash it. I work night shift and the last 24 hours are a bit of a blur. Sorry.'

Yvonne looks doubtful. 'If your hair's not clean it doesn't cut as well.'

'It's clean.'

With a new layer-cut, I meet Coral at the bike path.

'I like it,' she says.

'And it wasn't even washed.'

'You rebel.'

We start with warm-up strides. I ask her how work is, and she says she can't seem to do anything right.

'Maybe your boss is going through a rough time.'

'It's just *her.*'

'You could ask her.'

'She's my *boss,*' says Coral, as though this disqualifies her from being human.

'She's still human.'

'Okay, okay,' she says, looking at me. 'What's eating you?'

I start pumping my arms as we up the pace. 'There was an Irish ring on the breakfast table. Claddie or something.'

'Claddagh.'

'It wasn't mine.'

'Uh-huh.' Coral's puffing like a freight train, darting looks at me like a seagull. I know those looks. Her eyebrows squeeze together and her eyes almost clench. It's her 'I-can't-believe-you-stay-with-him-why-don't-you-leave' look.

'I know.'

'Well? You won't break, you know. You deserve better.'

'It's not that simple.'

'It isn't?'

'We've loved each other since we were 16.'

'*You've* loved *him*, you mean.'

'Okay, there's your answer.'

She doesn't reply.

'You alright?'

She's sweating more than normal. Pale.

'Just low on energy lately,' she says, slowing to a stop. 'Mind if we turn back?'

When we get to the carpark she leans on the bonnet of her Mazda 2. 'You know, I've never been happier with anyone than I am with Vince. The boys love him too. I feel like I've, you know, *come home*.'

'What do you mean?'

She plucks a leaf from under the wiper blade. 'Home is somewhere familiar,' she says, finally, 'somewhere safe. I don't know how else to say it.'

I think about this for a moment. I have half of it right. Steve's familiar. But safe?

'It's really not that difficult,' Coral says. 'You don't have any kids. Just tell him you don't want to be treated like second-hand furniture anymore. Then leave.' Her cool, damp hand is on my arm. 'Sounds corny, but you've only got one life and it's fucking short.'

At the time I thought the tears were overdoing it, but I wasn't to know, and neither was she, that a shadow was gnawing at her lung. It was to take her within four months.

Sitting straight-backed in his smart shirt, 13-year-old Jared is stoic. Young Joshie's shoulders are shaking. His dad reaches over and gently draws his head towards him.

Vince gets up to speak. Never in my life have I seen a man lay his heart wide open like this.

He turns to the coffin, tears coursing down his cheeks. 'I love you, Coral,' he says, and to everyone in that packed room he declares, 'After we moved in together, the first time I came home to see Coral and the two boys I was so happy I cried.'

Behind him the screen relays images, some grainy and old – Coral as a toddler, twirling a backyard hose towards the camera. Coral as a long-limbed 12-year-old in micro shorts. The most luminous of all is Coral on the beach in oversized sunglasses, big red smile, arms circling Vince's neck, sun on their faces and it's right there that I see happiness.

It's just after I've switched to day shift a few months later that Steve announces he's enrolled in a night course in woodworking. He feels stale, he says. He used to like making things as a boy – what happened?

'Why now, just when I've gone to days?' I'm mashing potatoes for shepherd's pie. My dad's coming over.

'It's not my fault. Just panned out that way.'

'You could have discussed it with me.'

'Do I need your permission?'

'You know what I mean.'

I spread the mash over the beef and make gridlines with a fork. 'Hon,' I say, 'I just thought we could start going out again – a pub here, a band there.'

'Bit old for it, aren't we?' Steve flicks on the telly.

'What?'

'Well, look at you, for example. Can't help noticing the gravity effect.'

'You're no oil painting yourself.'

I think of the photo at the funeral. Coral and Vince shining in the sunlight. Smiles broad as the earth. Crow's feet and all.

Over the Sara Lee, Dad's getting emotional. It happens from time to time. He's lost two wives to cancer. First my mum. Then Val. He and Val were so in love. You could hear her giggling in the bedroom whenever they stayed the night. It was Dad prancing around in his Y-fronts singing 'I Did It My Way' that set her off, she confided.

Despite his grief, Dad's doing well. He plays bowls, goes to church, grooves to swing time at the club. But from time to time, in spite of himself, the tears well up.

As soon as Dad pulls out his hanky, Steve leaves the table. It's State of Origin night.

'I'll get you a tea, Dad.'

'Thank you,' he says as he wipes away his tears. 'Thank you. Sorry.'

'It's okay, Dad.'

I look over at Steve. He's crouched towards the telly, his hands clenched.

While Dad's brushing his teeth, I prepare the guest bed and slide the hottie down the end where his toes can find it. He'd cheered up after dinner and insisted on doing the dishes. I even coaxed a song out of him. Steve turned up the volume on the TV.

'Thank you, darling,' Dad says as he eases under the covers. 'Now, off you go. Don't worry about me.'

I climb onto the space beside him and lean back against the bedhead. 'I don't feel like watching the footy tonight.'

He adjusts his pillow and puts his glasses on the bedside table.

'I'd rather talk for a while,' I say, 'if you're not too tired.'

I come sharply awake in the middle of the night. Dad must have pulled the doona over me and then fallen asleep with the light on. I stare at the ceiling, untangling myself from my dreams — one in particular. Except I realise it wasn't a dream. It was something Dad told me earlier. He said that when he and my mother went through a rough patch in their marriage, he'd been attracted to someone in his office. She was flirty, unattached, funny. But there was too much at stake, he said. He'd never have forgiven himself. I was shocked to hear he'd been so close to having an affair. Now I lie here wondering when and how I've become so immune to my partner's betrayals.

I watch my father for a moment. It's odd the way the tiny muscles in the waking face inform character. In sleep there's a falling away, an absence. I imagine him dead. I hold my palm a couple of inches from his nose, reassured by the warm, steady puffs of air. Maybe I'll stay here a little longer. It's the first time since Steve and I got together that I've ever chosen to sleep in another bed.

I slide deep into dreams. Nothing disturbs me until the front door opens and closes. Six-thirty. I listen to Steve's van back out of the driveway, do its half-turn and rev off into the dark. I realise this has been my first test of survival.

I've passed. And, just as Coral promised, nothing is broken.

Brand Worthy

Anto reaches down from the couch for a cigarette and lighter. He knows I hate him smoking in the house but what can I say when he asks if I'd rather he smoke dope? The creases on his cheek suggest he's been asleep for hours. I take his cereal bowl from the floor and hand it to Rachel.

Rachel's kindness, unpredictable sparks of wit and ready acceptance of me were the things that drew me to her when we met on a Business Administration course. Why she stuck by Anto though, I had no idea.

'Brand loyalty,' Rachel said, when I asked her.

'And what brand might that be?' I retorted, draining my canteen coffee. 'No Frills?'

Softie she may be, but Rachel's no walkover. Just before our graduation she told Anto he needed to work things out on his own. I chose that moment to suggest she and I share a house and was thrilled when she agreed.

We chanced on this great terrace in Glebe, and despite the age gap – Rachel is five years younger – we got on famously. We found steady work, watched old comedy collections, frequented the Retro club, and (very occasionally) got trashed. She taught me to cook; I taught her to clean. She seemed to like and trust me and for this reason I liked her even more.

After six months, Anto contacted Rachel to say rehab had changed his life, and she agreed to see him again. He was out of work, she told me, but he was clean, and after a while she asked if he could 'stay for a bit'.

I wasn't super keen, but said okay, as long as it was *just for a bit*. I didn't want our precious friendship ruined. And I didn't want to see Rachel hurt.

I'm a claims officer at an insurance firm in Ultimo. I like that it's not too challenging. I'm quite comfortable with things that are black and white and slightly dull. Requests that I take on more responsibility are usually greeted with thanks, but no thanks.

One day I'm working late on a report I've neglected to finish when the new security guy pops his head over the divider and scares the hell out of me.

'Leaving in a jiffy,' I say, wondering how 'jiffy' has suddenly become part of my vocab. Security Guy gives me the willies. There's a certain intensity in his eyes I can't quite work out. I lower my head and tap madly at my keyboard. Eventually he moves off to check the window latches, even though the windows are closed because of the air-con.

I just want to finish this report, chuck it on the boss's desk and leave. I could have finished it at home, but the shirtless Anto makes me heave. It's the clutch of wispy dark hairs at the base of his bony sternum, his small cherry nipples, and the smell coming from his armpits, his groin, or both. *Just for a bit* has turned into a month, two. He's brought home a stray cat. He's still unemployed. As far as I'm concerned, Rachel's being taken for a ride. Why can't she *see* it?

Security Guy's crashing round the kitchen. It's not his job to clean so there's no need for this. To my dismay he brings me a coffee.

'Kind of you,' I say, 'but I don't drink it late in the day. Keeps me awake.'

His expression changes to one of disappointment and…what, exactly? Again, I can't put my finger on it. I hold my breath, thinking he's about to snap, but all he says is, 'You're the boss.' He says 'boss' in a slightly narky way, like that doorman in *Seinfeld* Season Six who thinks everyone thinks they're better than he is: 'Why waste time making small talk with the doorman?'

He takes the cup back and I lower my head again. The report's flowing well and looking swish and professional. I'm bolding table-headings and creating bullet-point lists when I sense him behind me.

'I hope you don't mind,' he says. 'I have this fascination for data.' His voice is soft, hesitant.

'Uh-huh.' I nervously direct the cursor to the print menu. I wonder if he can hear my heart thumping.

'Random figures transformed into meaning,' he mumbles, 'in our utterly random world.'

I grab my daypack and move to the printer, slipping on my joggers as I go. He's following me. I can hear his keys rattling. He's a big guy.

'You're not scared, are you? I hope you're not scared of me.'

Don't they all say that just before they slit your throat/push you over the cliff/bolt the dungeon door/unzip their fly?

'Nope! Not scared. Not a bit. Gotta go.'

I toss the printout onto the boss's desk and make a beeline for the lift.

'See you tomorrow,' Security Guy calls.

I'm perched on a kitchen stool watching the evening news past the sight of Anto's unwashed feet, when his loathsome cat leaps onto the bench. I roar. It jumps down and stalks off, nose in the air, like a kid pretending a smack didn't hurt.

This damn cat. A week ago, excited by my progress with cultivating herbs in our little courtyard, I'd decided to make pesto, splurging on overpriced pine nuts and parmesan, only to arrive home to find the cat spraying the basil with its vile piss. I yelled blue murder and launched my foot at the planter, upturning the lot – cat, soil, basil and all. The cat scampered to the top of the ancient brick thing that used to be a barbecue and sat blinking its golden eyes at me like a Pharaoh's cat.

So, there's the cat issue. Then there's food. When it was just Rachel and me, we used to pool our pay every fortnight to cover rent and a massive shop. We ate the same sorts of food. The system worked. And even though Anto eats like a sparrow, I hated the thought that Rachel was supporting him and his scrawny cat. I suggested we split the fridge – Rachel and me with one section and Anto the other. That way we could see where his dole money was going. Rachel said this was selfish. I explained that it was Anto who was selfish and that he was using her (and me), and anyway how did she know that his grand plan wasn't to brainwash her and strip her of her wealth?

'What wealth?'

'All your accounts. It's wealth to him.'

'He's not interested in my money.'

'How do you know? How can you trust him?'

She looked at me with something like pity and sorrow. 'I just do.'

I'll try growing mint, I decide. It's indestructible. Put pepper on the soil to foil the feline.

The TV weather report says we're in for a scorcher of a summer.

'Lucky we've got the pool down the road,' Anto says, wriggling his filthy toes.

I make a face behind his back. How *dare* he say 'we'?

At work the next morning I notice the windows are open.

'Why are the windows open?' I ask Joshua, the new guy. He shrugs and continues to scroll through the photos on his camera.

'Have a look at Rupert in the run on Sunday.' He brings the screen to my eyes. 'Buffed abs or *what*. That man.'

Did Security Guy have something to do with the windows? Was it an excuse to hang around and breathe down my neck again?

I want to smother Anto's quivering fingers with sackcloth. I want to take his Bic lighter and singe his chest hairs. He listens to 'Sympathy for the Devil' over and over again. I can hear the 'woo-woos' coming at me through the floor of my room. If I drill a hole directly above where he sits on the couch, over his head, I could slowly drip something like Metho or turps onto his greasy mat of hair. We've had leaks before. He sometimes stands under them – to cool his brain, he says.

I have to work late again on another last-minute report. Security Guy is closing windows, rattling his keys. The soles of his shoes are thick rubber. He moves silently, like the space between thoughts. I watch him out of the corner of my eye. He presses the lock on each window three times. Each unoccupied chair receives three taps before being carefully aligned beneath each desk. Creepy.

Joshua is getting ready to leave. He's tidying his desk, the prettiest desk in the office: photo collage, dippy bird, magnet for paper clips – pinks and greens only – Wedgwood coffee cup with a gold rippled rim.

'Josh.'

'Hmm?'

'Can you wait a sec until I'm finished?'

'Sure, hon.'

I press print and hurry to the machine. Security Guy glances at me, poised to say something, but I whisper to Josh, 'Let's get out of here.'

'So, what was *your* father like?' Anto asks me out of the blue, as though he's just spent the last few minutes telling me about his.

'He was…flabby. Wore brown a lot.'

'I mean his character.'

I shrug. 'In a word, absent.'

My father's study had the best view in the house. My mother had rooms of her own, too. Kitchen, laundry. These rooms kept them apart. My bed-room kept me away from both of them. Two beds and just me.

It resurfaces in the media from time to time, usually when a child goes missing. It was my fault. My sister had trusted me, and whoever had coaxed her into the van. I was supposed to walk her home from school, not yell at her to leave me alone while I hung around the milk bar, hoping to run into this boy I liked. She was never found. The scumbag was never brought to justice.

My parents hated me for failing to protect her. And hated each other for the intimacy that had produced us both. We all hated the scumbag for taking her. Most of the time I hated myself.

Rachel walks in and perches on the sofa arm, looking at us with the hopefulness of a new pet. I want to tell her that she needn't think I'm warming to Anto simply because we've exchanged words. I still believe his agenda is to live off Rachel's kind heart and purse, and that she'll end up dumped like a kitten in a well.

'What have you two been talking about?'

'Our fathers,' I say, 'who art in... You off out somewhere?'

She's scrubbed and fresh in a clean white shirt. This is usually Anto's AA meeting time-slot. Rachel and I get to hang out together. She cooks, I clean up, we slob on the couch in our PJs with some wine and a DVD.

'I'm off to a meeting too.'

'What kind of meeting?'

She hesitates. 'Al-Anon.'

'What's that?'

'It's for people who have an alcoholic in their family.'

'He's not your *family*.'

'Friends too, it means. Not just family.'

Anto stands to tuck his shirt in, then reaches for Rachel's hand.

'*Good* friends,' he says.

The evening following the father question, Anto and I are watching the news and they're on about the Catholic Church and its many sins. The words seem to slip out of him by accident. He tells me he was once an altar boy. From my perch on the kitchen stool where I'm dipping into a pot of strawberry yoghurt I make surprised eyes and wonder whether to respond. Instead, I make him an offering. 'I think the office security guy is a serial killer.'

The news report shows the Cardinal at a press conference, speaking against a background of muted grey-green. Instead of reacting, Anto says, 'The priest didn't get me to suck him off or anything.' He takes a drag on his cigarette and shifts a cushion to one side.

'That's a relief,' I say, not sure I want to hear what's coming next. I take another spoonful of yoghurt, eyeing him warily.

He flicks off the TV and stares at the floor. I'd go off about the ash drifting onto the floorboards, but I'm stumped. I can't stand the guy and yet he seems poised to tell me something excruciatingly painful, private.

'Serial killer, eh?' he says. 'What's the giveaway? Severed fingers in the office freezer? Fondness for fava beans?'

I hoot a relieved laugh and wave my spoon about. 'Oh, I don't know exactly. I just find him creepy.'

Anto has showered, and cooked Eggs Florentine. He has laid places for three. He has swept. He wears shoes. All this makes me uneasy.

Rachel beams and looks at Anto and me in turn. I shatter the illusion of this familial triangle, by saying I intend to get a dog. My gaze slides off my plate towards Anto's cat. I swear its ears pricked up. Rachel's face falls. She glances at Anto. This is it, I think. Does she support and defend him or me?

'Anyway,' I rush on blindly, 'there's a guy who has a sign up at Zaman's.

He has a litter. I haven't had a dog since I was 12. I cried for weeks when he got run over. I want to walk a dog, pat a dog, take a dog to meet other dogs, buy dog treats from the produce store.' I love the produce store. I'd love to curl up in the corner of my room on a downy pet bed. Have someone bring me my bowl every morning. Brush my hair.

Of course, my master plan is that a dog will upset Anto's cat, which will in turn upset Anto. I *do not* trust him, and I want him gone. He's muscled in on our girl–girl domain. Rachel and I haven't watched a *Seinfeld* episode in months. I don't remember the last time we laughed. I'm so watchful and alert I could get a job with ASIO. Anto should be arrested for infiltration.

Silence has fallen. We eat our eggs. The yolks are sungold. Spinach sticks to our teeth.

Security Guy's weird habits and silent shoes have entered my dreams. He's locked me in a cell with one high, barred window and a computer. I spend my days keying in *pi*. Every three minutes he turns the key in the lock three times. He brings me bowls of soggy spinach.

I decide I need a new job to flush him out of my dreams. Each afternoon after work I cold-call employers. Note pad and pen alongside me on the kitchen bench.

'Could you keep it down while I make some calls?' I say to Anto. 'I would return the favour, only you appear to want to remain terminally unemployed.'

He's given up attempting a comeback. I am as acerbic as a grapefruit.

Rachel confronts me in the kitchen. 'You've made your point.' She picks up the Wettex and starts feverishly wiping the benches.

'Say what?'

She rinses, squeezes, wipes again. Her cheeks are flushed. 'Can't you let up on Anto?' she says, turning to me. 'What's he ever done to you?'

'It's what he's doing to *you* that's the problem,' I snarl.

Rachel looks at me like she's only really seeing me for the first time and what she sees leaves a bad taste.

We have a mint jungle. The cat is thwarted. And when I bring Bernie the Maltese-cross home from the litter man, the cat rears up like a snake, hissing.

Summer arrives, burning along the footpaths and under our door. The house is an oven. One Saturday afternoon the heat has buckled the grid or something, or maybe too many people are using air-con. We are without power. Rachel is visiting her mum and when I come downstairs even Anto's gone. I'm wilting, and Victoria Park pool seems like a good notion, so I grab my swimmers and head out into the furnace.

It's mayhem. Kids ignore the lane ropes, bobbing up in front of me, frog-kicking with their slippery learners' limbs. Two boys bomb the deep end, their plump brown waists glistening in low-slung board shorts.

After a few laps I check the pool clock and see Anto under the Hypoxic Blackout sign. Bobbing just below the rim of the pool I study him where he sits on a small ragged towel with his narrow chest, his hip bones sticking out above his boardies. His hands are cupped on his lap and his eyes are closed as he draws oxygen and sun into his body through his uplifted face. I imagine him swimming under water, oxygen levels plummeting, carbon dioxide overloading. Blackout. Leaving me alone with Rachel again. I'm suddenly aware of his eyes on me as if he knows what I'm thinking. He lifts his palm in greeting. I pretend to be unfogging my goggles, then swim away.

After my laps I towel myself dry on a patch of grass at the other end of the pool. Seems everyone's had the same idea today. I've nodded to the guy from the bottle shop and spotted Lisa from the Co-op, when someone

I recognise catches my eye. I can't quite place him. He's trying to inflate a child's arm floaties. The boy is in a blue rashie and saggy little Speedos and he's prodding the top of the man's head with his finger and erupting in bubbles of laughter every time the man snaps an air-bite.

While this fun game is in progress the inflating is going nowhere. I still can't place the man. Finally, the floaties are on and the man takes the boy's hand and leads him to the pool steps. On the way he stops to tap the bubbler three times and at the steps he does the same to the railing. All this while, the boy keeps his hand snuggled in his dad's and pays no heed to these small delays.

I can't look away. Little starfish hands reach for his dad's waiting palms as he kicks and kicks. Determination on his grim red lips. His eyes blink under flying droplets. Blue tiles glimmer beneath his orange wings. There are gasps of triumph when his father twirls him in the sunlit water.

It's too late to pretend. Security Guy has seen me. I sit up, put on my hat and go to the edge and say hello. He says hello back. I tell the boy how great he's doing and that his dad seems very proud and pleased. And then I get my towel and bag and put on my sandals and say goodbye, see you Monday.

The footpath burns beneath my feet. Above me leaves curl, shucked of moisture. People drift in and out of shops and the air shimmers. There's a tarp over the produce in the fruit shop to prevent it from cooking.

When I get home the electricity's on and there's a message on the machine about a casual job with a car rental company. I erase it.

His name is Jeremy. By the end of the week I've discovered he has trouble reading faces and emotions. Working in security is perfect because it doesn't involve too much social interaction. He's on his own with his little boy since his wife died a few years back. Her parents live nearby and they dote on their grandson. Jeremy drops him off at theirs three days a week.

On the weekends he and his son are stuck together like glue.

'I might see you both at the pool again sometime,' I say to Jeremy.

Anto is volunteering three days a week at the Salvos. It's a bit of a surprise. Rachel is distant. Thoughtful. Our lease is up in a few weeks and I'm terrified she might say she wants to find a place for her and Anto – without me. I clean the house from top to bottom. I stock the fridge. I buy two exotic tapestry-covered cushions from the antique store and a pot of vanilla-scented heliotrope in the hope she'll realise what an irreplaceable flatmate and friend I am. Anto says in passing the place smells nice and Rachel says it's clean, without meeting my eyes.

My lovable dog Bernie has been trying to befriend the cat, but the cat can only spit, lash out and disappear. The cat is now rarely seen.

'Not my fault,' I say to Anto, 'if your cat is antisocial.'

'It's a *cat*,' he says, shaking his head. 'Bernie is a *dog*.'

One day, after a particularly gruelling day in claims world (customer number 11 declares he's been driving the same route for 43 years and there's never been a stop sign; customer number 14 blames windscreen damage on galah smashing its brains out), there's no Bernie to greet me when I open the door. I call and call. I check upstairs. I go out the back. No Bernie.

Minutes later Anto walks in and I bail him up: 'Where's my dog?'

'I dunno,' he says. 'Pay day today, so a couple of hours ago I went out for some smokes. When I got back he was gone. Thought maybe he'd squeezed under the gate. So I went back out—'

'Oh, right. *Dole* day.' I look at him with what I hope is a withering stare. 'Tell me what really happened.'

'What do you mean?'

'Am I next? You going to put a sack over my head and dump me in the harbour?' I'm getting so worked up my eyes feel like they're throwing sparks. Anto pushes his hair back and opens his mouth to speak. Nice try at a bewildered look, I think.

'All part of the grand plan, isn't it?' I barrel on. 'You'll have Rachel all to yourself. With no one to see you suck the goodness out of her.'

Anto holds his hands in front of him in a gesture of defence rather than surrender. 'Calm down,' he says, which is like a red rag to a bull.

I can feel spittle in the corner of my mouth. I must look hideous, but I can't stop. 'And what happens to *me*?' I cry. 'Where does that leave *me*?' I can't help the crack in my voice.

'Mate, you need to chill,' he says. 'There is no plan. Rachel's…amazing. I love her. I would never hurt her. And believe it or not, I like you too.'

'Liar!'

'Okay, listen,' he says. 'I'm going out again. I'll leave you to it. Make yourself a cup of tea or something.'

'Yeah, off you go – dog-killer!' I splutter. I collapse on the couch and grab one of the new cushions and bury my face in it.

The front door opens. 'Get lost!' I yell, without looking up.

'Sup?' says Rachel, dropping her keys on the coffee table.

'Oh, hi.' I sit up and wipe my eyes. 'Anto's got rid of Bernie. How many times have I told you that guy is no good?'

Without a word, Rachel puts a carton of milk in the fridge. She comes back to stand by the couch. 'So you think Anto has, what, killed your dog?'

The minute she says this I know how crazy it sounds, but I nod, sniffling like a child.

Rachel counts my slurs on her fingers, one spike at a time. '*Loser. Hopeless. Alco.* And now *Dog-killer.* Oh, and *No Frills*, let's not forget that one.'

My chest feels cold. I bring my fists together to warm it up. Unmoved, Rachel marches to her room and closes the door. She doesn't do slamming.

I curl up in the corner of the couch, clutching the cushion. After a couple of minutes, I stop snivelling and take a few deep breaths. This is not the time to succumb to hypoxic blackout in any shape or form. I've well and truly stuffed up. Not for the first time.

I flip open my laptop and design a LOST notice.

At the sound of the thumping printer, Rachel's door opens. She looks at me guardedly.

I hold up one of the notices. 'I was wrong. Totally and unforgivably wrong. Anto is not a dog-killer. There is a gap under the gate. I've been meaning to block it off. I'm the loser. Hopeless. Not Brand Worthy.'

'Don't forget No Frills.'

'That too.'

Rachel picks up the pile of notices. Then she opens the bottom kitchen drawer and takes out some tape and scissors. 'Yes, Brand Worthy,' she says. 'Minimal repackaging required. Merits prime position. Come with me.'

I follow meekly. We head into the evening streets and tape notices to telegraph poles and shop windows. Every dog I see sets me hoping. Bernie is not streetwise, nor is he particularly brave. The cars and buses and people would scare him witless. I'm also on the lookout for Anto and am mentally preparing an apology. I can tell Rachel is on the lookout too.

Back home Rachel and I cook vegie pasta together, leaving enough in the pan for Anto. The cat purrs round our ankles. By 7:30 we've had no lost-dog calls and no word from Anto. Rachel has gone quiet. Anto will be back soon, I tell her, I'm sure. I'm concerned for him too, since he's not much better than a stray himself.

We try watching the 'jockeys versus boxers' *Seinfeld* ep, but even Kramer with his 'I'm out there, Jerry, and I'm *lovin* every minute of it!' barely raises a smile.

All of a sudden, the cat stiffens and scuttles under the TV console.

The door opens and in walks Anto, a bundle in his arms. It's a giant plastic cone, with Bernie's snout quivering like a cube of liquorice in the centre.

'Oh, my Bernie boy,' I cry. 'What happened?' Lifting the blanket, I see a freshly shaven leg and a stitched-up gash.

'I tried to tell you earlier,' Anto says. He takes the dog and settles him into his velour bed. As I kneel down to scratch his head, Bernie reveals the lower whites of his eyes and shudders, full of self-pity. The cat seems to sense the lack of threat and sits a short distance away, casually nuzzling a paw.

'When I got back from the shops I realised Bernie was missing,' says Anto, 'so I went looking for him. I found him in Derwent Lane and took him straight to the vet. Came home to tell you.'

'Oh, God,' I say, in a tiny voice. I can hardly meet Anto's eyes. 'How did you pay for it?'

'*Dole* day, remember?'

I nod miserably. 'You must have blown the lot.'

'Yep.'

'I owe you.'

'Yep.'

'Anto, I— '

'Anything to eat?'

'Oh,' I say, cheering a little. 'Yes. There is. You must be starving.'

I bustle about in the kitchen, filling a bowl with hot steaming pasta, and dropping cutlery on the floor in my haste. 'Glass of iced tea? Ginger beer?'

Rachel puts a hand on my arm. 'It's okay. Anto's cool. He really is. He forgives you.'

Anto twines his fork through the fettucine. 'Cop a look at those two.'

Rachel and I turn to see the cat rumbling a low purr and tucking its paws beneath its chest to settle alongside Bernie's bed. Bernie lets out a long, contented sigh, licks his chops a couple of times and closes his eyes.

At the sight of poor little Bernie's cone and the aloof cat settled in like an old friend, I start to laugh. I can't remember the last time I laughed like this. And as I'm laughing Anto's index finger circles his temple, signing *she's mad* to Rachel. Rachel nods a little too vigorously and this sets me off again, spluttering and choking. Rachel joins in and soon we both have tears streaming down our cheeks as we collapse in the kitchen, holding each other up.

Anto takes another mouthful of pasta. 'We're living in a madhouse,' he says to the animals. 'You know that, don't you?' He chews for a moment, leans back in his chair, grinning and says, 'Yep. It's a bloody madhouse.'

Now, Voyager

Charlotte's mother tightened her grip on her cabin bag as they waited to check in.

'Intolerable,' Charlotte heard her mutter.

In front of them a girl clutching a panda was flicking the barrier tape against the metal pole – *clink, clink*. Conscious of her mother's growing irritation, Charlotte gave the girl a friendly smile. The child spun around and buried her face in a long black skirt. I repel her, thought Charlotte. I must look like an ugly colossus to someone so tiny. But at least the clinking's stopped.

'Do you think Darren will attend the funeral?' she said, to distract her mother. The last time she'd spoken to her brother he'd said, 'Why do you put up with it? She takes advantage of you. It's no life.'

Her mother spat a puff of air. 'I doubt even Darren can answer that.'

'The line is moving, Mother. We have to move along.'

Behind the counters, the check-in clerks in their red uniforms flashed brisk, clean smiles. Such confidence! Their hair pulled tightly into French rolls, or clipped and slicked away from unblemished skin. So easy, bright, efficient, capable. Young.

'In any case,' Charlotte's mother went on, 'I don't suppose I'll have much to say to him.'

Darren had been sober for years. Surely it was time to make an attempt.

'Your sister will be a comfort,' said her mother.

Yes, Julie had always been a *comfort*.

'Next.'

Charlotte placed her mother's suitcase on the scales.

'Any damaged goods, scissors, knives, explosives, aerosols?'

Damaged goods? She'd misheard. *Dangerous* goods. Damaged goods she might have declared. Seventy-five kilos' worth under this dun coat.

Weight-check and tag. Charlotte's bag followed her mother's along the conveyer belt and under the flap like an obedient hound.

With her erect posture, dressed in navy court shoes and matching gabardine coat, her mother appeared tired but defiant. Her hair was set in iron-grey waves and her thin skin stretched tight across her cheekbones. After the security check, Charlotte would take her to a café. The waiter would bring a stainless-steel pot of tea and an oversized muffin. Charlotte would accept her mother's payment.

'I hope those people have our suitcases.' Her mother peered out the cabin window at the baggage handlers below.

'We checked the labels. Twice.'

'Did you pack my pills?'

'Yes, I packed your pills.'

'No need to snap.'

Again, Darren appeared in Charlotte's mind. She felt as though she'd come to a fork in the road. She was unable to decide which route to take and needed her brother's help. She stowed her handbag carefully under the seat in front of her. It was a relief knowing that the little box it contained had made it past security. She'd left her pocket knife locked in her desk drawer at home.

A pregnant woman moved slowly past, grabbing the backs of seats.

Charlotte tested the button on her armrest, reclined her seat an inch, and brought it up again. Her mother waved away the cabin earphones for both of them.

An ice-cream-smeared boy squealed down the aisle. Hot on his heels was a man with a tumble of brown hair, dressed in jeans and a cornflower-blue t-shirt. He gathered up the squirming boy and at his apologetic smile Charlotte blushed and looked down at her lap.

Click, click. The slim flight attendant with pressed pants and manicured hands moved down the aisle shutting the overhead lockers.

'Ma'am, seat in the upright position please,' said another attendant alongside.

Charlotte's mother looked disapprovingly at his ear stud, then at his badge. CRAIG.

'Mother, lean forward while I put your seat up.'

Cabin crew, please arm your doors and cross-check.

'Are you planning to speak at the funeral?' asked Charlotte.

'We haven't discussed the program yet,' said her mother.

'I just thought – Aunt Evelyn was your only sibling.'

'I'm well aware of that. She was a dear sister.'

The plane lumbered away from the gate, engines at a low hum. Next to Charlotte, the man in C smelt of hamburger. The hairs on the backs of his hands stood up like hog bristle, and it was soon apparent he had the habit of following each sniff with a short, dry cough.

Continue to breathe normally…fit your own mask first before assisting others.

Craig's tanned fingers held the mask to his face. So, she would have to fit her own before helping her mother.

There are eight emergency exits.

Craig pointed to the rear, sides and front of the plane. Charlotte turned to check the exits behind her, and the escape path lighting along the aisle.

The aisle and exits must be completely clear.

The man in C was ignoring the safety demonstration, swiping up and down his phone, his elbow prodding Charlotte's.

Cabin crew, please take your seats for take-off.

The plane taxied to the head of the runway and came to a stop. Her mother's knuckles were white as she gripped the armrest.

'Are you alright, Mother?'

'I never liked flying.'

'You flew all over the world with Father.'

'It was expected of me.'

The engines kicked into high gear with an urgent, insistent whine. Charlotte's mother opened her mouth soundlessly, shut it again. Charlotte's heart thumped as the plane picked up speed, faster and faster, before raising its nose into the sky. They were airborne. Next to her she heard a sharp inhalation.

'Are your ears hurting? Can I get you a lozenge?' She reached down for her mother's handbag, snagging her watch on her stocking.

'No,' said her mother, kicking her hand away. 'I don't want a lozenge. I don't want you to touch my handbag.' She looked down at the loose thread on her stocking and pounded her palm on the armrest. 'I don't want anything, I tell you.'

Charlotte sat back in silence.

'Evelyn said the consolation in having a late child, especially a daughter, would be the comfort she would bring me in my old age. It's a mystery to me how you are bringing me comfort. And still so clumsy.'

The man in C sniffed and coughed. For a moment the green, vinegary odour of pickle hung in the air.

Through the window, past her mother, as the plane angled towards the sea, Charlotte could see the red roofs of the sprawling suburbs. An Olympic pool, without swimmers. A long, yellow beach. The never-ending ocean, flecked with white.

The drinks cart drew up alongside. Charlotte wanted a whisky. She knew her mother would disapprove. The woman across the aisle had just ordered a Bloody Mary.

'Whisky, please,' she said to Craig.

'Tea,' said her mother, firmly.

Charlotte paid and took the small plastic tumbler, together with a napkin and salted nuts. She laid down her mother's tray and passed her the tea. She tossed the whisky down. 'It sounds as though you never wanted me, Mother.' The drink fired her throat.

'Is that what I said?' Her mother stirred her tea with the plastic spoon.

'What else would a child think on hearing that?' said Charlotte, her heart thudding against her ribs.

'Child?' her mother said, scornfully. 'You're 43 years old. Time you grew a thick skin.'

The whisky slid its heat into Charlotte's veins. 'Another, please.' She signalled to Craig. 'No ice.'

'You'll get tipsy,' said her mother. 'And you can't disguise the smell.'

Charlotte leant her head back. The passenger behind her pushed at her seat, lowering their tray.

'I've disappointed you though. You've made that clear.'

Her mother didn't reply. She wouldn't unless it suited her.

Charlotte unclipped her seat belt.

'Where are you going?'

'Bathroom.'

Charlotte made her way unsteadily down the aisle, excusing herself to the slim flight attendant as she squeezed past the trolley.

The lavatory was in front of the handsome dad and his son. The man was flipping through the in-flight magazine above the boy's flushed face, resting in slumber against his thigh. He looked up at Charlotte, and she smiled a smile that she imagined would send his son running for cover.

She scary, he would say.

'Over-excited,' said the man, indicating his son, 'on his first flight.'

She nodded and backed into the bathroom. She took the box from her handbag, opened it and threw the bits of plaster down her throat. She washed her hands and wiped the hand basin. Then she unlatched the door with a flutter of nerves to see the dad again, but his eyes were closed.

Her mother and the man in C were also asleep. He grunted and shifted his legs for Charlotte to pass. She listened to the steady drone of the plane. Must be halfway there by now. Passengers slept, read. Some stared down the aisle or fiddled with their phones. Bloody Mary was doing a Sudoku. Charlotte leant across to peer out the window at the densely vegetated hills, dusted with snow.

'I can't breathe,' said her mother.

'Sorry,' said Charlotte, pulling away.

'No. I mean I can't *breathe*.' Her mother tugged at her collar, which was buttoned to the neck and fastened with an antique brooch.

'Here, let me help.'

Charlotte unclipped the brooch and loosened her mother's blouse. She fanned her with the magazine. 'Is that better?'

'Not really.'

'Can I get you anything?' It was Craig. He smelt of gardenia.

Charlotte's mother opened her eyes. 'Water.' She moaned and pressed her ribs. 'Something hurts right here.'

Charlotte reached up to twist on the air-conditioning.

'That won't do any good.'

'Here you are, ma'am.' Craig had returned with a cup of water and a napkin.

Charlotte thanked him and held the cup to her mother's lips, fuchsia lipstick embedded in their creases. She dabbed the napkin at a stray drop on her chin.

'Not so *hard*,' said her mother, with a cough. 'You always did have a heavy hand.'

Charlotte was reminded of her mother's thin fingers arranging roses on the walnut hall table. Careful, precise.

In the evenings Charlotte used to creep around corners to sneak leftovers. Anything. Take them to her room. In bed she picked at the wall beside her until eventually the pale, striped wallpaper tore and exposed the plaster, which crumbled at her picking finger and one night she tested a piece on her tongue. Swallowed.

'That's enough,' said her mother, pushing away the cup. 'Let me be.'

Charlotte took the cup and wedged it into the seat pocket in front of her.

'Has the pain gone?'

'No,' said her mother, with a wince. 'I'm extremely uncomfortable.'

There was a disturbance up ahead. Charlotte craned her neck to see Craig fussing over a passenger. She glanced at her mother. Her eyes were closed. Hands clasped in her lap.

Another flight attendant joined Craig then disappeared into the kitchen area, returning with a water jug and a towel. What was happening? Might it be a birth? How exciting. A baby born on the plane. Charlotte strained to hear over the drone of the engines. Was that a cry? No, only her mother whimpering in her sleep.

Perhaps they'll call for a doctor or a nurse. She could put up her hand, saying, 'I was a nurse.' They needn't know she'd been dismissed after barely a year. She still remembered words such as *febrile, arrhythmia, intubate*.

Charlotte played it out in her head. Slippery baby in her hands. Blue cord. The heaving little chest. She would wrap it in an airline blanket, gently clean its eyes and nose with a moistened tissue. Place it on the mother's breast...

'What are you dreaming about?' Her mother's sharp tone.

...place it on the mother's breast. Watch the cat-mouth open and seek. Help the mother direct her dark nipple into the tiny pink cave. Those initial sucking noises. The slip off the breast. She would hold the back of the baby's head and clamp the mouth wide around the areola. The mother's expression an intent mix of rapture and anxiety, followed by relief and a twinge of pain.

'You look as silly as a wet hen,' her mother said. 'Take that smile off your face.'

'You seem better,' said Charlotte.

'I have a dreadful headache. Call for a tablet.'

'There's some sort of emergency. They're busy.'

'Well, I can't see a thing. When are we going to arrive? My legs are beginning to cramp. You needn't think you can be of any use, you know,' she said, 'if it's a medical emergency. Is that what you're hoping for? Is that why you look ridiculous and excited? You'd be nothing but a hindrance. You never had the gift. Nursing wasn't for you and you weren't for nursing. Matron made it plain.'

Charlotte's big knees were wedged behind the seat in front of her, reclined to its limit, its occupant asleep. LIFE VEST UNDER YOUR SEAT.

'You didn't fit in. You weren't efficient and adept. You with your clumsy feet and hands. You needed fine motor skills. You needed to be good with *people*. You needed a bedside manner. You didn't have the temperament, I'm afraid. You didn't—'

'Didn't, couldn't, didn't, couldn't,' Charlotte said to the back of the seat. 'How could I ever succeed at anything? How could I?'

There was a short silence.

'And then, of course,' her mother's index finger stood to attention, 'there was your habit.'

Charlotte stared ahead.

'You needn't think I don't know about it. I know about it. I've known about it for years. *Years.* The little patches on the walls. The way you're always hunting for suitable walls. That little pocket knife you keep in your handbag. Yes, I know about that too. You'd dig. And dig.'

Charlotte's nails pressed into her palms. Her mother's voice in her left ear. To her right the odour of a man who was pretending not to listen. He kept flicking at his trouser leg, at imaginary lint. Sniff, cough. Someone was screaming. Or was it the jet engines?

'You hunted for it, didn't you?'

Who was screaming? The man next to her wouldn't stop. Sniff, cough. Flick, flick. She put her hands over her ears.

'Where's the oxygen mask? I can't breathe. I can't breathe.'

Charlotte was lying between the escape path strips. Someone slid a small pillow under her head. She looked up to see Craig's mauve tie and wing-badge. His dimpled chin.

'Most-eventful-flight award,' he said, with a giggle. 'First the little boy, now you.'

'Little boy?'

'Yes. Tossed up the delightful contents of his tummy on our divine upholstery.'

'So there was no new baby born on board?'

'Now that *would* be award material.'

She tried to sit up. 'My mother—'

'Don't move,' said Craig. 'Your face is the colour of my butt-cheeks.'

'But—'

'Your mother is as happy as a pig in clover. She's got a whisky in hand and ABC 1 in front of her on the screen.'

Charlotte sank back down. 'I'm in the way.'

'We've finished service, hon,' said Craig. 'Just stay there until we start our descent.'

Charlotte stared at the aircraft ceiling, feeling the plane vibrate along the length of her body. The floor smelt faintly of cleaning fluid and coffee. In an emergency, she thought, they would need to ensure the exit path was clear. Craig has taken care of Mother. Craig says I'm not in the way. Bloody Mary looked down and smiled. Charlotte lifted her fingers in acknowledgement.

She thought of Darren. She simply must talk to him. She lay still, waiting to hear the clunk of the aircraft wheels as they prepared for landing. Until then, she would not move.

Buoyancy

Natalie tiptoes into Carla's room. Her daughter's arms are flung above her head and a tiny foot has snuck out from under the covers to cool. She creeps out. At the front door she slips on her joggers, and as she breaks into a run the streetlights shut off.

When she returns, Carla is at the breakfast table with Peter. She must have woken early. He's still in his t-shirt and boxers.

'Look, Mummy,' says Carla, as she plunges the knife into the peanut butter and drags it across her toast. 'Daddy didn' help. Not one bit.'

'You need to be careful,' Natalie says, bending to kiss her daughter. 'You can get a nasty cut from a knife.'

'Yuk. You hab to hab a shower,' says Carla, wiping Natalie's sweat from her cheek.

'Yes, you're right. I'll go and have one now.'

'Good run?' asks Peter.

'Yep,' says Natalie over her shoulder.

Natalie steps into the jet of hot water, planning the day ahead. She'll drop Carla at preschool, then drive on to work. Three weeks to deadline, the mood in the office is still peppy.

Towelling herself dry, Natalie examines the skin on her belly. Having a baby loosens the body. Tightens or loosens a relationship.

Carla barges into the bathroom. 'Mummy, I wanna wear my red overalls.

Daddy says they're in the wash. He says I got to wear my green leggins. I – don – wan – to.'

'Well, if your red overalls are in the wash, it's because they're dirty,' says Natalie, rolling on deodorant. 'Your green leggings are clean and you look like an elf in them.'

'I wan my *red overalls*.'

'Alright, then.' Natalie sighs. 'Tell Daddy to get them from the laundry.' She closes her eyes as Carla's 'Yay!' trails down the corridor. Parents are supposed to unite on child-rearing issues. Peter has said this often enough.

She's buttoning up her shirt when Peter appears at the bedroom door.

'Didn't we agree not to give in to her?'

'Didn't we agree one of us should always watch her?' she retorts. 'Maybe it was different when you were three years old – so many older siblings to take care of you in your big, happy family.'

Peter's lips tighten as he turns to go.

In the kitchen Natalie sips her tea as she brushes Carla's hair. Peter, in a clean shirt and tie now, drops his sports bag on the floor.

'Don't forget I have training after work,' he says. 'How about the two of you come and watch?'

'She needs to be in bed by 6:30.'

Peter pushes his fingers through his hair. 'One late-ish night won't hurt.'

Natalie tosses the dregs of her tea down the sink. 'It messes up her routine. We're supposed to stick to a routine. I've been reading up on it.'

'Come on,' he urges, moving towards Natalie. 'It'll be good for both of you. And me.' He places a hand on her waist. 'Carla will have a hoot running along the sidelines with the other kids.'

Natalie twists away from him and reaches for Carla's hand. 'Not this time. Let's go, sweetie. We're running late.'

At the office Natalie settles down at her desk, unclogs her inbox and gets to work editing a feature on green city living. A regular contributor – the writing is nice and clean.

Bec, the chief-sub, tall and loose-limbed, pops her head over the divider. 'Given it some thought?' she asks.

Bec's been urging Natalie to join her in the summer season of ocean swims. For Natalie the definition of swimming is a pool and a solid black line, a clear view of the bottom. Besides, she needs her running. That quick exit before Carla wakes. The firm surface underfoot. Time alone. But Bec is forever raving about the joy of the sea, the deep blue beneath, beyond. The expanding self.

'Still considering,' says Natalie. 'Hard to get away.'

'Peter's hands-on, isn't he?' says Bec. 'Do you good,' she adds. 'You seem stressed, lately. No offence.'

For two days Natalie works from home. Carla, a misery of itching and fever with chicken pox, follows her, clings to her. Her high-pitched whine shreds Natalie's nerves. In the afternoon she switches on *In the Night Garden* and pours herself a glass of wine. She should probably lie down and sing to her daughter. Isn't that what good mothers do?

Loud voices. A sound, hard and soft, like a rock thrown on sand. A cry like a shore bird, bleak and short. She opens the door. Her father's face. Its passionfruit skin. Lips thin as a ruler. Beyond, her mother, face turned away. Her mother runs to the bathroom. Her father glares at Natalie as though she disgusts him and without a word leaves, slamming the front door on his way out.

Natalie tries the bathroom door handle.

'Mummy.'

'Go away.'

'Take time out,' says Peter, when he gets home. 'I'll look after Carla. Go for a walk. Clear your head.'

'I'm okay.' Natalie tops up her glass and nods at the package in Peter's hand. 'What's that?'

Peter pulls out a bottle of Pinetarsol. 'Your mum says it goes in the bath. It's supposed to soothe the skin. Stop the awful itching.'

Natalie slams her glass on the bench. 'You rang my mother?'

'For advice, Nat,' says Peter, peering at the instructions on the bottle. 'She wants to help.'

'Pardon? Can't remember her being much help when *I* was a kid. Leave her out of it, please.'

'Give her a chance.' Peter puts the bottle down and looks at Natalie. 'She has a grandchild now. And she's frail.'

'Frail! Hah. That's rich. She shouldn't have dined out on painkillers all those years.'

Peter reaches out and touches her arm. 'Your father was the arsehole, not your mum.'

'And how did she deal with it?' Natalie opens the Pinetarsol and recoils at the smell. 'She checked out, that's what.' She thrusts the bottle back into his hands. '*You* put it in the bath, since you know so much about everything.'

Do it! the ocean-swim flyer urges Natalie from her desk. She clicks on the website and examines last year's photos. There are green, pink and yellow caps for the different age groups. Bodies of all shapes and sizes waiting on the sand. Faces glowing, laughing. Photos of the water, the foamy frenzy of the start, the glittering path to the first buoy, an underwater close-up of a swimmer's pale legs, nothing but the darkest of blues beyond. It comes back to her then, the way she'd swim in the local pool after school, hour after hour, just to delay going home to get her mother up and dressed, fed. In the water she had no responsibility for anything or anyone. Solitary and weightless. Only the sound of her own breath.

She taps her finger on the mouse and frowns. Almost without thinking, she clicks on the drop-down menu and pays the entry fee. She can always pull out. No one need know.

'You've registered.' Bec is behind her chair with a coffee.

'Mmm.'

'Fantastic. We can train together at lunch.'

Natalie spends the next half-hour editing. Not responding to emails. Ignoring the phone.

Natalie tucks her hair under her cap, lines her goggles with spit. Bec suggests they start with a six-lap warm-up, then increase their speed. They take adjacent lanes. Bec swims with smooth, powerful strokes. Natalie's heart rate ramps up as her arms turn over. Soon she slips into a familiar rhythm – three strokes then a breath, three strokes then a breath.

She runs to her room. No one looks for her. She emerges when it's dark and tiptoes to the kitchen. Her mother's cheek is fat. She serves Natalie boiled egg but forgets to cut the toast into fingers.

After the sixth lap she pulls up, puffing. Bec is grinning.

'Nice style.'

'Thanks,' says Natalie. 'You're fast.'

'You'll overtake me soon enough – with a bit of training.'

At the end of the session Natalie's arm muscles are burning, but it doesn't matter. When her head is under the water the world disappears.

She buys a new racer and goggles. One morning she drives to the beach before work and ventures beyond the breakers. She glimpses the endless blue Bec spoke of. As the seabed falls away, panic ripples through her. She hugs her knees to her chest, then catches the next wave back to shore. The following morning with Bec by her side she feels braver. Together, they swim headland to headland.

It's deadline week and the office is in a frenzy. Faces frown at computer screens. Someone whoops. Someone else curses. They take turns to fetch pastries, chocolate, coffee. And then they're in the zone – silence apart from the quick tapping of keyboards.

By seven o'clock Friday evening the pages are off to press. Bec produces wine and they all cheer. They abandon the carnage on their desks.

As the swim draws closer, it's as though Natalie is a warrior woman. She flexes her arms in the bathroom mirror. Her stomach is firm and defined. Before work she practises diving under waves; at lunch she swims laps of the pool. Soon she starts training after work, too. Stroke over the long black line. Turn at the wall. Stroke over the long black line.

When Peter collects Carla late from preschool, Natalie calls him unreliable.

'Well, where are *you*?' he says. 'You're always swimming. We never see you.'

The two of them had met at the Woodford Folk Festival. Natalie was almost fainting from heat when out of nowhere someone handed her a cup of ice-cold water. She looked up into the kindest eyes she'd ever seen. Now these eyes are hard and narrow.

'You keep telling me to take time out,' she says.

'Yes,' says Peter, 'but do you realise I haven't been able to go to *my* training? And Carla has been asking why you don't pick her up or eat dinner with us anymore. We're a family in case you've forgotten.'

'Oh, I see. Is that what we are? A family. I didn't recognise it. I thought family was defined by five kids and a ramshackle home full of wrestling and noise and banter and mashed potato and parents who adored each other.'

Peter looks at her. 'Nice one,' he says, taking Carla by the hand. 'Come on, honey, bath-time.'

It's the day of the swim. Sky and water are clear. There's a small swell. Beyond the breakers the water shines. The big inflatable orange buoys are in position. A helicopter circles. Bec and Natalie stand side by side on the beach in their age group of green caps. Bec chats and jokes with the other swimmers. Natalie is quiet, focusing on the water.

The hooter sounds, and they race for the sea. As Natalie takes her first dive an arm thumps her head. She coughs on a mouthful of foam, gasps, stands to adjust her goggles, then dives under the next wave. For what seems like forever there's nothing but white noise and spray, limbs thrashing on all sides. Adrenaline surges through her. She keeps swallowing water. Then all at once the waves are behind her and the bottom is out of reach. The water is muscular. The swimmers begin to separate, fan out, and her breathing settles. She lifts her head to check the position of the first buoy, and when her head re-enters, the water's blue shadows have replaced the sandy bed and it's endless. No black line, no walls.

The swimmers converge at the first buoy. Someone pulls on Natalie's leg. She kicks fiercely and swims away.

Her father never returns. The last pockets of tenderness in her mother shrivel into chunks of pain that demand prescription after prescription.

By the time Natalie has rounded the final buoy she feels she could swim forever. She powers on, catches a wave all the way to shore and pants up the sand to have her number checked off.

Bec pats her on the back. 'You did it! How do you feel?'

'Great.' The shortest word she can muster.

'Guess what?' Bec says, with a grin. 'There's another swim next weekend – 2.4 *k*s.'

Natalie gives Bec the thumbs-up. She could swim her life away.

She looks around for Peter and Carla and spots them at last out on a rock platform, peering into pools. They missed her finish. She shades her eyes. With them is a woman in a broad-brimmed hat. Despite the thin frame Natalie recognises her. Bec hands her a slice of watermelon and when she looks back the woman has gone.

'What was *she* doing there?' Natalie asks Peter that evening.

Peter's cutting up Carla's fish fingers. Carla, freshly bathed, is jumping on and off the couch in her red dressing-gown singing 'Wheels on the Bus'.

'I asked her to join us,' he says, quietly. 'She's very proud of you.'

'You had no *right*,' says Natalie.

'Carla has a right to see her grandmother.'

Natalie takes the plate from him. 'It's my business, not yours. I don't want to see her, and I don't want Carla to.' Her voice rises.

'Sh,' says Peter, gesturing towards Carla.

'...go roun' and roun', roun' and roun', roun' and roun', wheels on the bus go...' sings Carla, louder and louder. Up she jumps and down she jumps.

Natalie slams the plate down. '*Stop*, Carla! Stop that awful noise! Stop jumping. And you,' she yells at Peter, 'don't you dare tell me to shush.' Spit flies from her mouth.

She sees Peter's fist clench, his lips go thin as a ruler, his face with its passionfruit skin.

'What do you want?' she cries. 'You want to hit me? That's it, isn't it?' She presents him with her cheek. 'Go on then, *hit me.*'

Carla has stopped singing. The little figure in the red dressing-gown has wedged herself between her parents, pushing at Natalie, crying, 'Stop, Mummy, stop, *stop.*'

That night Carla calls out dozens of times – 'water', 'toilet', 'I'm hot,' 'I wan' a puppy dog'. Finally, Natalie screams, 'Go to sleep or no more *In the Night Garden.*' Carla's cries escalate until she's sobbing for Daddy. Peter goes to her, strokes her forehead until she calms. Natalie stares at the ceiling.

Later, when both are asleep, Natalie sneaks in to curl at the end of Carla's bed. Her daughter's breathing stutters through her blocked nose. The bedcovers smell of sweet talc and spilt milk. Above her, Natalie can just make out the mobile of cut-out stars wrapped in silver-foil that Carla made at preschool. She gives it a nudge. It bobs and twirls. After a while she stands and pats the covers back into place. Rather than return to bed she tiptoes to the lounge room, where she dozes on the couch until dawn, then grabs her swimmers and drives to the beach.

Dark clouds line the horizon. Sand stings her legs as she sprints to the sea. She wades out, stumbling a couple of times on the uneven sand-banks, pushing her thighs against the tug of the water. A set of dumpers approaches. She ducks under the first, a roaring in her ears. She gulps for air and dives again, and again, until she is beyond the waves, out in the clear, cold sea. She treads water for a moment, then swims parallel to the beach, breathing to the left, so she can admire the glimmering horizon. As the sun begins to climb above the clouds she finds herself on a sandbank. She stands up, holding herself against the wind, watching the ocean catch fire as the sun rises higher, and then without warning the bank collapses, plunging her into a deep, roiling channel. Her legs spiral. Her arms flail. The rip sucks her out towards the sun. She struggles, shocked and frightened, her breath coming in gasps. The shore is suddenly a long way away. She keeps struggling until she decides to stop. She closes her eyes, relaxes her muscles, submits. Nothing. Nothing but the sound of the sea.

'Give me your hand.' The voice seems to come from the deep. 'Up here, give me your hand.'

A blue surfboard. A plaited bracelet on a firm, tanned wrist. Clean fingernails. Natalie drifts, swirls.

'Give me your hand,' the girl repeats, in a voice like thousands of pulverised shells.

Natalie opens her eyes again, sees tiny blond hairs on the smooth arm reaching for her.

'Leave me alone,' she hears herself saying, shutting her eyes. 'I'm okay.'

'Come on,' persists the girl. 'Lift up your arm.'

A silver waterfall of hair. Clear eyes locking on to hers. Natalie's arm is leaden. She wills it out of the water, towards the sky, takes hold of the offered hand. This hand hauls her up until she's lying on the surfboard, half-in, half-out of the water. The girl tugs Natalie's left leg and flips it over the board in front of her, swivelling her body so it's stable.

The wax is sticky under Natalie's cheek and smells faintly of coconut. She opens her eyes and whispers a thankyou. The girl shrugs it off.

'Trained to do it,' she says, swinging the nose of the board around effortlessly. 'Not the best day to be out swimming,' she adds. 'Lucky I decided to get a surf in before school.'

Natalie pushes herself up on her aching arms to focus on the approaching shore. The wind sheers past her ears, filling her lungs with clean air. She grips the sides of the board as the girl takes a wave, barrelling them towards the sand.

The Bridge

Jarrod's mum pulled in to a servo. Jarrod remembered how the family used to park in a rest area with a putrid drop-toilet and wooden tables strewn with gum leaves and ants. They'd devour homemade sandwiches and cake and fruit and shoo off magpies. There'd be a bin crammed with rubbish, and an old couple drinking tea in silence beside their caravan.

Before long a Fanta and a sausage roll appeared at the car window.

'Don't make a mess.'

Jarrod ribboned the pastry with tomato sauce. 'How much longer?' he said, as his mum got behind the wheel.

'First words you've uttered in over an hour,' she said. 'You okay?'

Jarrod wished she'd stop asking.

Last week of holidays before high school. Jarrod wasn't keen. What if the kids were weird nerds who didn't do sport? He was the only one in his group going to the selective. His mum said he had to make the most of *the opportunity*. On orientation day she pointed out the trophy cabinets: 'Look. They do sport here,' she whispered. His dad would get it. 'If you don't want to go, don't,' he'd say.

Now she's pretending to be happy – switching stations on the radio, humming. She inhaled and then let out a long sigh. 'I can smell the sea!' Her smile used only her mouth.

Jarrod rolled his eyes before turning to stare out the window.

The floor of the cabin was like plastic, so you could walk around with wet, sandy feet. One bedroom with a double bed. A fold-out sofa in the lounge. Jarrod's mum said they could share the double, but Jarrod said he'd take the sofa.

She placed a soft brush near the entrance. 'Clean the sand off your feet whenever you come in.'

Jarrod spent the first day circling the holiday park on his scooter. Watching dads herd their children together for the beach. He discovered a creek that emerged from the scrub and wound into the lagoon – a hang-out for the older kids, who dangled lines over the edge of the old bridge, hurled rocks into the deep channels, built dams. Jarrod continued on his way the minute anyone gave him more than a casual glance.

'Having fun?' his mum would call from the cabin's shadows when he returned. She'd hand him a few dollars to go to Reception, which doubled as a shop. 'Get some milk and a treat for yourself.'

The concrete ramp outside Reception was monopolised by a girl with a purple penny skateboard. She'd balance carefully, gripping the handrail, then release and speed to the bottom with a squeal. Tucking the skateboard under her arm she'd repeat this over and over.

Reception man would curve his long neck round the screen door like an emu, wiggling his shaggy eyebrows and cheering the girl on. Reception woman, big-boned and heavy, her hair dyed a rusty black, would snap, 'You're in the way. People need to get past. Go play somewhere else.'

On the second morning, Jarrod was charged with buying tea bags. He scootered past the cabin verandahs rainbowed with towels and wove his way round tough, wiry banksias that offered little shade. As he neared the shop a boy raced up on thin brown legs, calling, 'Ebony, come *on*. Dad says we're going to rent a canoe. Come *on*.'

'One more,' said Ebony. 'Please, Christopher?'

Reception woman's head materialised at the screen door. 'Off you go, girlie. You've skated enough now.'

Just as Ebony tossed her a wave, her skateboard overshot the ramp, throwing her off balance so fast she could only gasp. Jarrod saw her head whack the handrail and then her legs scoot over the edge, yanking up her green denim shorts to expose the tan line. He noticed bits of green polish on her toenails. One of her thongs tumbled into the dust.

Jarrod and a cluster of onlookers stood by as Ebony's father scooped her up and into his car and then Christopher hopped in and they skidded off way faster than the park speed limit.

His mum was relaxing on the tiny verandah with a glass of wine. Jarrod sat on the step, watching the old guys from the fancy tent set-up prepare their rods and buckets for the evening's fishing. Somewhere a baby was bawling, and he could smell frying sausages.

He licked a strip of sunburn on his wrist. 'Just off to the bridge,' he said, standing up.

'Want me to come with you?'

'Nah, that's okay,' said Jarrod. 'It's not far.'

'Take your jumper. It's getting cool.'

Jarrod sensed her eyes on him as he headed off. It annoyed him that he was always her main focus. Life used to be noisy, busy. Friends to dinner. Energetic pot-stirring. Now the only person his mum talked to, apart from Jarrod, was Ginny. Skinny Ginny had taken over the swimwear shop and seemed to be forever talking about Funkita versus Speedo, F-cups, and add-ons like chlorine soap on the counter.

'You know what?' Jarrod overheard his mum say to Ginny one day. 'My husband has left me and I don't have a lot of money and I certainly don't have the energy to be discussing shop troubles whenever you stop by and never say no to a plunger coffee.'

From his bedroom, Jarrod stirred his mug of milk, chunky with Milo. He decided from then on that he'd only take one spoonful. His body felt heavy. Ginny was annoying but without her visits he was afraid his mum would go quiet again. At these times, part of him wanted to run away, and part of him wanted to ask if she was okay.

In sight of the bridge now, Jarrod saw Christopher bent over the railing, staring at the water. Jarrod hung back beside a gum laced with scribbles.

Without warning, Christopher raised his head. 'You in high school?' he called.

Jarrod ran his fingernail down the trunk. 'I start next week. You?'

'Going into Year Six.'

Overhead, three black cockatoos coasted south on high, mournful cries.

'Where is everyone?' asked Jarrod, edging forward.

'Someone saw a whale,' said Christopher. 'They all ran off to check it out.'

Jarrod stepped onto the bridge planks – salt-worn and bleached. The creek was the colour of his mum's tea. The boys' shadows wobbled on the water.

'How's your sister?' asked Jarrod.

'She got mild concussion,' said Christopher, 'and a broken wrist. She's in the cabin with Dad.'

Jarrod spied a tiny stud embedded in Christopher's left nostril and was so impressed that without thinking he said, 'Your mum let you get that?'

Christopher fingered the stud. 'Cool, isn't it? Nah. Don't have a mum anymore.' Suddenly he was all action. 'Listen, I've got to find Ebony's wristband. It's in there somewhere. It's orange.' He ran lightly across the bridge and down into the water. Jarrod followed.

Christopher told Jarrod he'd urged Ebony to take the wristband off –

this all-day carnival ride band that she'd been wearing since...well, for months – so that he could try it out as a sling shot. He'd finally got it off her that morning. Promised he'd give it back *and* buy her a bag of sour worms. But he'd accidentally flicked it into the water.

'I feel really bad,' he said. 'Especially now, after her accident and everything. Ebs said she was going to wear it until it "sintegrated".' He grinned at Jarrod.

Side by side the two boys waded slowly, swirling the water with their hands, turning over rocks, sifting mud. The air had cooled. Shadows lengthened, and everyone started trooping back from the beach.

'Getting hard to see,' said Jarrod, after a while.

'We can come back in the morning,' said Christopher. He straightened up and looked at Jarrod. His salty hair stuck out in all directions. 'Can you come back in the morning?'

Jarrod nodded. 'Yep, sure.' He felt his body lighten.

Jarrod looked up to see his mum on the bridge, her old cardigan hanging down below her shorts. He felt the urge to both fling himself into her arms and tell her to go away.

'Hello,' she said, brightly.

'Hi,' said Jarrod.

Still knee-deep in creek water, Christopher introduced himself. Jarrod saw his open smile, the way he told his mother about the wristband, and how readily and kindly she responded.

Thudding onto the planks now, Ebony and her dad. The girl gave a little skip and a run, followed by a loud, boisterous 'Hi-i-i!'

'Ebs, we're looking for your carnival band,' said Christopher.

'Oh, I don't need it anymore,' she said. 'I have *this*,' and she held aloft her arm in its lime-green cast. 'Dad says we can get the canoe tomorrow and I'm allowed to come even with this as long as I sit still and not row or anything. Do you want to come too?' She directed this question at Jarrod.

'Oh, wait. There might not be enough room. Hmm,' she said, pressing a finger to her lips. 'I know!' The finger shot up as inspiration struck. 'Two canoes. Can we, Dad?'

Jarrod and Christopher joined them on the bridge. Low in the sky the first star. Jarrod's toes alive with creek cold. Ebony singing and skipping. His mum's eyes crinkling at the corners, glancing at him, and at the others.

Jarrod moved to her side, just close enough to feel the soft fabric of her cardigan on his arm.

Feather

Paul cupped the egg in his hands. It was brown. And warm. Living in a concrete apartment block, he'd never have imagined holding a freshly laid egg. But earlier that afternoon, when Tanya had arrived home from work and said, 'Hey, I think there's a chook living in the basement,' Paul, barely lifting his eyes from the glossy pages of *Wheels*, could only bring himself to say, 'Okay.'

'What, you don't believe me?'

He looked up. Her hand rested lightly on her hip. Change the tone, son, he thought. She was in her sexy office skirt. Best play along.

'That's feasible,' said Paul, nodding. 'A chook.'

'Feasible, what are you a lawyer?'

Ah, the mood. She must have seen the speck of dirt in the doorway. And he hadn't changed the toilet roll. Better get to the bathroom before she did.

'Hey, I was talking to you.'

'Still listening!'

'I found it this morning when I was leaving,' Tanya called back. 'I couldn't believe it. This black feather beside my car.'

'Probably a magpie,' said Paul. 'Or a raven.'

'Okay, forget it,' said Tanya. 'You obviously couldn't give a toss. But it's only about the most extraordinary thing.'

'I do give a toss,' said Paul. He stood in the bathroom doorway, facing her, now. 'Sorry. Tell me about it.'

Tanya stared at him for a moment. Her hand fell from her hip.

'So,' she said, finally, 'after that − finding the feather − I could have sworn I heard *clucking*. But I was running late. I didn't have time to look around.'

Paul gazed at her. Her long stockinged legs. Mauve cotton blouse, still crisp. Stunning. 'Takeaway Thai tonight? Bottle of wine?'

'Did you hear a single word I said?'

'Yes,' said Paul. 'A farmyard fowl has chosen our basement carpark for its home.'

'We live in the city, for godsake.' Tanya waved her arms towards the window as if to remind him. 'How would a chook get in here?'

'Maybe it waddled in from Chinatown. Wait, that's a duck,' he said. 'Strutted?'

'Thing is,' said Tanya, ignoring him, 'if we find it we can have fresh eggs.'

She went to the bedroom to get changed. Paul wondered if he should follow her. Not the brightest idea.

She emerged wearing grey track pants and a t-shirt. Slowly but surely, his hopes for the evening were dissolving.

'You know what you are?' she said, pulling on her Ugg boots.

I bet it's not a super-hero, he thought. 'A super-hero?'

'An obstructionist.'

'Now who's the bloody lawyer?'

'You never simply agree or embrace an idea without finding some sort of obstruction.'

'Why should I blindly accept everything you decide to say or do?'

'It'd be nice if you just once said "brilliant idea" or "yes, let's do that".'

Paul clicked on the news and flopped on the couch. He sensed a gloom settling over them, like fallout. Disappointment lurked just under his skin. Hers too, he imagined. Lately, he found himself wondering how to manage The Extrication. Not what he *really* wanted, because, this time, for the first time, he'd let down his guard. He'd allowed someone in.

He fixed his gaze on the TV screen, as though his life depended on interest-free periods at Harvey Norman.

The apartment door banged shut.

She's gone to look for the bloody chook. Let her. He lay back against the cushions and flicked channels.

Tanya strode along the corridor to the lift. The block was new, the carpet still spongy and clean underfoot. With the scarcity of city rentals, it was a lucky find. Two bedrooms. North-easterly aspect. Moving in together seemed the obvious next step. They'd been dating for 10 wonderful months. Until Paul, Tanya's relationships had ended badly – either continuing past the use-by or ending in betrayal. Nasty. At 32 she'd had enough. So, for once she laid her heart on the table, and to her surprise Paul grew tender. When they talked about one day having a baby, his voice cracked. They decided to move in together. That was a year ago.

Tanya pushed the button and waited. Kirsten, from 101 and heavily pregnant, joined her.

'Hi,' said Kirsten, puffing.

Tanya nodded hello. She wasn't really in the mood for chit-chat after the chook argument. She stared at her reflection in the lift's twin metal doors.

Kirsten pressed her hand to her side, wincing.

'Much longer?' asked Tanya, reluctantly, standing aside to let Kirsten enter.

'Due any day now,' said Kirsten. 'Can't wait.'

'Really? That's gone fast.' Tanya watched the numbers count down.

'I'm just off to buy some olives,' said Kirsten, as they stepped out. 'Can't get hold of Jake and I'm desperate. Cravings, you know?'

'Yeah,' said Tanya, although she didn't.

'See you later,' said Kirsten, sending a beep to her silver Honda. 'Nice to chat.'

Tanya stood for a moment, alert for chook noises. She dropped to her knees to look under the cars, feeling vaguely ridiculous. What if there really *was* a fat bundle of black feathers and a pair of beady eyes? She hadn't really thought this through. How do you even pick up a chook? Do they bite?

Still kneeling, she saw a familiar pair of tan lace-up shoes step out of the lift. Fawn trousers, slightly frayed, with a neat crease down the centre. It was Ron, the widower from the second floor. Tanya shuffled backwards on all fours, out of sight.

What's he up to? she wondered, watching Ron make his way across the carpark to the fire door. Where's his walking stick? What if he falls and cracks his head?

The roller-door to the carpark clanked up to let the silver Honda through, wet with rain. That was quick, thought Tanya. She watched as Kirsten heaved herself out of the car, a jar of olives in her hand. She looked pale.

Tanya waited for the lift to close, then crossed to the fire door.

Sitting on his own in front of the TV was lonely. Paul kept seeing KFC ads. Dead chooks. This got him thinking about live chooks. Then about women. Life. About getting a grip on it. He decided to go and find his girlfriend. See if she'd found this chook.

He stepped out of the lift. No sign of Tanya. No sign of a chook. He was about to head back up, when he heard voices – one clearly Tanya's. He followed it to the fire door.

'I named her Rosie, after my dear wife,' Ron was saying. In his arms was a plump black hen, looking quite comfortable, darting its head back and forth on its little neck. 'Found her a couple of weeks ago when I was putting the garbage out. Pets are against rules, so I've been keeping her in here. I don't know what else to do with her. Hello there,' he said to Paul.

'G'day, Ron.'

'See?' said Tanya. 'Told you there was a chook!' She grinned at Paul, stroking Rosie's glossy black feathers.

Just look at her, thought Paul, admiring Tanya. She's all lit up.

'Don't worry, she's not cooped up all day,' said Ron. 'I take her out the back for a bit of a scratch when everyone's at work. I clipped her wings,' he added, with a touch of pride.

Paul reached over and stroked the feathers. Soft sounds came from the hen's throat. 'This is one happy chook.'

'We always kept chooks,' said Ron, his face creasing into a smile.

'Any eggs, Ron?' asked Tanya.

Before Ron could answer, they heard, 'Hello, Tanya? Are you still here? Can you help me?'

Tanya and Paul exchanged glances, then raced across the carpark to find Kirsten doubled over by the lift.

'I think the baby's on its way.' Kirsten screwed up her face. 'I've left Jake a message. Here's my mobile. Could you keep trying him, please?'

'Which hospital are you booked into?' said Tanya, as she took the phone.

'Home birth. Actually, can you call my midwife first? Under Josie.'

Paul put his arm out to support her. 'Let's get you upstairs.'

Kirsten groaned again. 'They're getting closer.' She grabbed hold of Paul, screwing up her face. 'Aagh, shit, shit, shitty, shit.'

'You'll be okay,' said Paul. 'Breathe. Just focus on your breathing, Kirsten.'

He's so calm, thought Tanya, as she waited for the midwife to pick up.

'First level?' asked Ron, who by now had left the chook behind and made his way over.

Kirsten nodded.

Ron pressed the lift button. The doors were about to close when a blue car sped into the carpark and a tall man in a suit leapt out.

'Jake!'

Jake jumped into the lift and Kirsten clutched his arm, squeezing so hard the tendons on the back of her hand stood up. He took her hand in his. 'I came as quick as I could.' His eyes flicked from Paul to Tanya, to Ron. 'What's happening?'

'I reckon the contractions are about five minutes apart,' said Paul.

'Here you go,' said Tanya, handing Jake the phone. 'It's Josie, the midwife. Says she'll be here in 15 minutes.'

At level one the two couples stepped out. 'Thanks for all your help,' said Jake. He supported Kirsten down the corridor, phone to his ear.

'We'll let you know!' Kirsten called over her shoulder.

Tanya and Paul were left on their own. Ron took the lift back down to tend to the chook.

Paul slipped his arm round Tanya's waist as they headed to their apartment. 'Wow,' he said. 'I hope she's alright.'

'And the baby.'

'And the baby,' said Paul. He unlocked their door. 'You hungry? How about I whip us up a pasta?'

'Sounds good,' said Tanya, sinking down on the couch. She stared at her reflection in the blank TV screen. Paul poured a glass of wine and placed it in her hand.

'Cheers,' she said. 'You were great with her.'

'Thanks.'

'No, really great.'

'Just call me a super-hero.'

Tanya leant back, taking a sip. 'It's miraculous, isn't it? There could be new life in this building any minute.'

'Absolutely mind-blowing,' said Paul. He sat down beside her, clinked his glass to hers. 'Here's to the baby.'

'Yep. Here's to the baby.'

There was a knock at the door. They looked at each other. 'Already?' Paul jumped up. 'Can't be.'

It was Ron, standing at the door with a broad smile. 'Just laid,' he said, handing Paul the egg. 'First one.'

Paul took the egg. It was brown. And warm.

'Come on in, Ron,' he said.

Paul poured Ron a glass of wine and pulled up a chair for him. Then he went back to sit beside Tanya. He sat holding the egg, feeling the pressure of Tanya's thigh beside his. The three of them sat there as evening rolled into night, waiting to hear the news. While they were talking, Paul kept hold of the egg. He cupped it in his hands, keeping it warm for as long as possible.

Colin's Lemon

Dorothy waited in line at the bus shelter with her shopping trolley in the torpor of mid-afternoon. Through the windows of the approaching bus she could see the lively faces of high schoolers and hoped there'd be a seat.

Halfway down the aisle an angular boy mumbled and stood up. As Dorothy was sinking onto the seat with relief, panic seized her. She'd forgotten to buy the all-important lemon. Oh, just this once would Colin be content without? Surely chives from the garden would do. Chives might add an interesting flavour. She wouldn't say a word about the lemon until the fish was in front of him. Not that she was frightened, but there was just no knowing, and even after 50 years, *50 years*, Colin was unpredictable.

Ettie said Dorothy was so accustomed to this unpredictability that if Colin were ever to be magnanimous and forgiving, she wouldn't know what to do with herself. The thing was, mused Dorothy, Ettie's outlook was tinged with an alert suspicion ever since her husband's bowels had twisted up in knots. Ettie's opinions were to be taken with a grain of the proverbial. Nevertheless, these chats often unsettled her. It was almost beyond imagining, a life without Colin.

She reached into her bag and pressed the fish in its wrapper. Still cool. It was a nice, plump snapper. It should please Colin. Damn shame about the lemon. What had she been thinking? She checked her watch. Should she go back? But it was so very hot! What she'd give for a cup of tea.

She pushed the buzzer. 'Driver, I'd like to get off,' she called, hauling herself up.

The driver's arms were stretched across the steering wheel. He shot Dorothy a puckered glance of impatience in the mirror. 'Pulling out, ma'am,' he said. 'You can get off at the next stop.'

'But I forgot to buy the lemon,' Dorothy exclaimed.

The driver held her gaze.

Somebody behind her snickered.

The doors hissed open.

Dorothy descended into the blazing sun.

The 50 paces to the greengrocers felt like 500. Shopping was taking the stuffing out of her lately, but Dorothy was reluctant to sign up for home delivery, since truth be told it was nice to be out of the house.

Lemon purchased (75 cents – highway robbery), she trudged back to the bus stop. What an awful afternoon. The fish could go off in this heat. Her head throbbed. The shelter was full. No one stood up for her.

It was five o'clock when she finally stepped through the door and crossed into the living room.

Next to the stepladder and a can of WD-40 lay Colin on his back with his mouth open. The ceiling fan squeaked overhead. Dorothy waved a hand over her husband's glassy eyes. She leant down and pressed two fingers to his neck, recoiling at the odour.

'I bought you a lemon,' she said, loudly, 'to go with your fish.'

She reached into her trolley, pulled out the lemon and positioned it in the hole of Colin's mouth. 'There you go,' she said, with a nod of approval. 'Just the way you like it.'

Acknowledgements

When *This Person Is Not That Person* found its eventual home with Puncher & Wattmann it felt like the right fit. Many thanks to Ed Wright for accepting the manuscript. Thanks also to Dannielle Burke for asking the hard editorial questions.

A Varuna PIP Fellowship meant I was able to spend a fruitful and wintry week to work on the manuscript in an environment that honours the writer, and I am enormously grateful to the Eleanor Dark Foundation for this time.

I am grateful too to the Australian Society of Authors for awarding me a mentorship with the wonderful Janet Hutchinson, whose astute and carefully worded suggestions ('I'd be inclined to leave this one out') not only led to a more cohesive manuscript, but also to a new friendship.

To these fellow writers: Linda Godfrey, Ali Jane Smith, Fay Ryan, Elizabeth Hodgson, Andrea Gawthorne, I am indebted to you all. We share our food and homes, and keep each other writing. We urge each other on after setbacks and celebrate each other's successes. I am in awe of your brilliant and creative minds, nourished by your empathy and wisdom, and incredibly thankful for your feedback on these stories.

Thanks to Scotti and Alec who have enriched my life and who may one day read my words, and to Jill, aka Samantha, as always.

www.ingramcontent.com/pod-product-compliance
Lightning Source LLC
Chambersburg PA
CBHW031320280626
47169CB00019B/2333